Michaela stared in dismay at the photographs

If the picture of her and Keir in a passionate embrace fell into the wrong hands, she'd be crushed.

"I imagine you'd like the photos back," Keir said smoothly.

"Of course," she snapped, hope rushing upward. "Does that mean you'll give them to me?" She waited fretfully for his reply, knowing she'd been mad to expect it to be easy.

"Possibly. It all depends on you, Ms James," he said. "If you agree to my proposition, then you may have the photographs, and negatives, of course."

Michaela felt a tingle of apprehension. "And what is your proposition?"

"It's quite simple, Ms James. You may have all of them back if you agree to spend three weekends with me—here in this flat."

JENNIFER TAYLOR, Liverpool-born, still lives in Lancashire, though now in beautiful countryside with her husband and young son and daughter. She is a chartered librarian and worked for the Liverpool City Libraries for many years. She has always written and has cupboards full of unfinished manuscripts to prove it. When she decided to try romance writing, Jennifer found it far more challenging and enjoyable than her other efforts. She manages to fit her writing in her busy schedule of working, running the house and caring for the children. Her books contain a strong element of humor as she feels laughter is an important part of a loving relationship.

JENNIFER TAYLOR

final score

Harlequin Books

TORONTO • NEW YORK • LONDON
AMSTERDAM • PARIS • SYDNEY • HAMBURG
STOCKHOLM • ATHENS • TOKYO • MILAN

Harlequin Presents first edition May 1989
ISBN 0-373-11173-8

Original hardcover edition published in 1988
by Mills & Boon Limited

CHAPTER ONE

SIX out of ten . . . it seemed a low score, but then she hadn't managed to snatch a look at the others yet.

Shifting slightly in the high-backed seat, Mickey edged herself closer, casually tilting the wide brim of her blue felt hat upwards to give her a better view across his bent arm.

For nigh on half-an-hour the man had been writing, the bold, black strokes spinning briskly from the tip of his pen, fast covering several sheets of white paper, and she was intrigued. What on earth was he writing about?

Quickly she skimmed over the curls of black ink, taking a few seconds before her brain locked in to his distinctive script and she stifled a gasp. It was no shopping list, that was certain!

Melodie Greaves. Age 23. Height 5ft 7ins. Weight 120 lbs. Hair Blonde (Possibly dyed) Eyes Brown. Unmarried.

Legs	9/10
Figure	9/10
Hair	8/10
Teeth	6/10
Eyes	8/10
Dress	10/10
Intelligence	3/10
Personality	5/10
Cooking skills	2/10
Fondness for children	5/10
Grand Total	65/100

With widening eyes Mickey raced over each precisely documented point, automatically noting the scores and the total out of a hundred. Closing her eyes, she rested back against the hard cushion. Maybe she'd been wrong, maybe it was a shopping list, after all . . . for a new harem!

The steady rhythm of the pen moving unfalteringly over the thick white paper called to her as insistently as a snake-charmer's flute, and reluctantly she slithered a glance sideways, automatically pushing the huge, tortoiseshell-framed glasses more firmly up her nose. The long, tanned hand skated on across its paper rink and, fascinated, Mickey watched another score unfold, step by step. 87/100 . . . Not bad; obviously Angela was doing rather better than poor Melodie. She could hardly wait for the next one to appear; perhaps that would hit the nineties!

'Your coffee, Mr Grant.'

The polite tones of the air hostess stemmed the flow, and hastily Mickey turned away, afraid to be caught peeping.

'Thank you, just what I needed.'

His voice was low, deep, sending a delicious ripple of pleasure curling through her, and she shivered delicately. She'd read about dark brown voices, of course, but this was the first time she'd actually heard one. It made her toes curl inside the pointed confines of her high-heeled boots.

'Is there anything else I can get you, sir?'

The breathy tone to the girl's voice showed she wasn't immune to it either, and silently Mickey sympathised; a voice like that should be licensed with a double-O prefix—it was lethal.

'No, nothing at the moment, thank you,' the man answered, and the hostess moved away.

From the corner of her eye Mickey watched as he sipped at the hot coffee while he studied his notes, adding a word here, a phrase there, till he seemed to be satisfied he'd missed nothing. Slipping the cap back on to his pen, he shuffled the pages into a neat pile and stood up, easing some considerable length of long, muscular leg from between the close-packed rows of seats till he could turn round and settle the work carefully down on the cushion.

For a brief moment Mickey had a full-frontal glimpse of the strong features which had been tantalising her ever since they took off, and lost no time in taking stock. Sun-streaked, teak-brown hair fell loosely over a broad, tanned forehead, brilliant blue eyes glittered under heavy, dark brows, a thick, gilt-tipped beard framed a sensuously carved mouth . . . what a topping for a gorgeous, muscular, near six-foot frame!

Ducking under the low baggage rack, the man strode easily down the aisle and disappeared into the wash-room, and stealthily Mickey cast a look round at her other seat companion, an elderly lady who was dozing contentedly, before turning back to that tantalising sheaf of white so close at hand. She was just dying to get a closer look at those notes, but should she?

Briefly, for all of two seconds, she wrestled with the ethics of the desire before conceding defeat and snatch-ing up the thin fold of paper. Quickly she flicked through the pages, glancing at the name and down to the total, before passing on to the next. There were eight in all, and, as far as she could tell from her swift perusal, Angela was in the lead, though what the competition was for she hesitated to guess. Perhaps a closer study would tell her.

Carefully she worked her way through the pile once again, chuckling softly at some at the remarks he'd made. She could only hope he was more tactful to their faces than he was in print; some of the comments were little short of libellous.

'I believe those belong to me.'

A large, tanned hand appeared before her fascinated gaze, and with a squeal of alarm Mickey looked up. Glittering blue eyes burned angrily down at her, and wordlessly she handed him the thin fan of white, her hand trembling slightly, making the paper rustle like dead leaves.

With a barely controlled violence he snatched them from her, shoving them roughly into a leather briefcase, its smooth lid embossed with the initials KG, before slamming himself down into his seat, his back partly turned towards her.

For a brief moment Mickey toyed with the idea of offering her apologies; after all, it was unforgivable that she'd been snooping—and even more so that she'd been caught —but she quickly squashed the urge. Even his back looked angry, and she had the nasty suspicion she might be no match for him in his present mood. No, discretion being the better part of valour, she'd be well advised to leave both it and him alone for the time being. A pity, though; he was the most fascinating man she'd seen for ages, though she doubted if he felt the same fascination for her. Nervously she swallowed a small chuckle of laughter . . . she'd bet anything her score would be a big, fat zero!

A short time later the plane dipped in to land, and with a sigh of relief Mickey unsnapped her seat-belt, quickly gathering her huge bag and stack of magazines together. She'd be glad to get off, glad to get away from the waves of antipathy which flowed from that broad, muscular back. Warily she shot a look sideways, relieved to find he was already up and making his way down the aisle. She'd let him get well ahead, set a few people between them before she joined the queue to disembark.

Standing, she jammed the hat more firmly down on her head and looped the strap of her bag over her shoulder, her eyes still following his progress down the aisle. A tiny shiver raced through her body. She'd got off lightly this time, very lightly, but instinct told her that next time she wouldn't be so lucky. She could only pray there would never be a next time!

The queue for the taxi rank was impressive. Swiftly, Mickey counted heads and gave up when she reached twenty, tapping her foot with impatience. At this rate it would be after midnight before she got home, and Gerald would be justifiably furious. Quickly, she cast a look at the slim gold watch strapped to her wrist, and groaned despairingly; they would be holding the paper now for her column. Why on earth hadn't she telexed it through before she caught the flight, and saved all this hassle?

For a brief moment she debated finding a phone and ringing through to the office, but quickly decided against it. She'd passed the bank of telephones on her way out and their queues had been even more formidable than the ones for the taxis. No, what she had to concentrate on now was getting home just as quickly as possible, and just for a moment she regretted having refused Rob's offer to meet her. At the time it had seemed pointless to let him make a special journey out to the airport just to fetch her, but now, looking at the long, slow-moving trail of people, she wasn't so certain. There had to be something she could do, surely, something other than just standing here waiting, some sort of special tactic, maybe?

Thinking quickly, Mickey edged her way out of the long, patient line of weary travellers, and skipped smartly across to the island which divided the flow of airport traffic into two lanes, then waited impatiently until the lights of an incoming taxi split the growing darkness. Sucking in a few deep breaths, she took a tighter grip on the suitcase handle and clamped her elbow down over the bulging shape of the overstuffed tote-bag to keep it close to her side. This would be a tricky maneouvre, demanding her full concentration, and she couldn't afford any mishap which might alter her timing.

Heart pounding, she watched the taxi draw in to the kerb with a dry squeal of brakes. A tall figure, almost indiscernible in the grey-blue gloom of twilight, opened the back door, conferring briefly with the driver before stepping inside. The cab edged slowly forwards and she was off in a glorious, loping sprint, dodging between the stream of cars, ignoring the strident, abusive sound of horns. Getting level with the slow-moving vehicle, she grasped the handle, wrenching the door open and throwing herself and her case inside to land in an ungainly heap half-on and half-off the seat. Winded, she rested back, a contented smile curving her full lips. She'd done it, she was in; now, just one last hurdle to overcome.

Turning, she faced the silent occupant, her well-rehearsed little speech tripping quickly off her tongue.

'Oh, I'm so sorry, but it's rather an emergency. Would you mind if I share . . . Oh!'

With a little gasp of dismay, Mickey stared up into a pair of furious familiar blue eyes, surprise robbing her of any more words.

'Oh, please do. After all, you've shared so much of mine already, with difference will one more thing make?'

The carved mouth twisted sardonically inside its framing beard, and with an expression of horror on her delicate features Mickey leant back against the corner of the seat, silently cursing her bad luck.

Of all the cabs, in all the towns, she had to jump into this one!

The silence was so thick, it would have needed a hammer to break it.

Mickey kept her eyes forwards, locked on the driver's head. Carefully she arranged her bag on her knee, hugging it protectively to her like a shield. Her suitcase was resting against her legs, a sharp edge digging uncomfortably into her shin, but she ignored it. There was no way she was going to start wriggling around, drawing attention to herself; she'd rather put up with a little discomfort first.

Warily she chanced a glance in the man's direction, her eyes stopping, widening, when they encountered his. He smiled, if you could call the rather nasty curl of his mouth a smile.

'Well?' he queried.

How had she ever thought his voice attractive? The coldness of its deep tone sent a shiver of alarm along her nerves, and for an instant Mickey stared inanely back at him.

'Well, what?' she croaked out at last, her mouth suddeny parched.

'I should have thought that was obvious,' he snarled harshly. 'What the hell did you think you were doing on the plane, reading my papers? Have you never heard of invading people's privacy?'

Swallowing convulsively, Mickey stared dumbly back at him. In truth, she couldn't blame him for being angry, it had been a dreadful thing for her to do. The trouble was, she just couldn't understand what had possessed her to do it in the first place, let alone find a satisfactory explanation to give him!

'Cat got your tongue, then?' he snapped, and she struggled to answer.

'I'm sorry,' she stammered nervously, desperately trying to get her quivering jaw under control. 'Really I'm awfully sorry . . . I don't know what came over me. I was just . . . well, just overwhelmed with curiosity to see what you were writing. It's never happened before, and quite frankly, it will never happen again.' She stared back at him, hazel eyes pleading for him to accept her apology.

'So you don't make a habit of it, then? It's not one of your usual little quirks?'

'No,' Her voice was as low and miserable as she felt, and she sank deeper down the seat.

'Just plain old-fashioned curiosity, then. But be warned, you know what that did to the cat, don't you?'

There was an almost threatening note to his harsh voice, and Mickey shivered. Why had she ever tangled in his affairs in the first place? There was a ruthless quality about him which she found strangely intimidating.

'I'm sorry,' she repeated quietly, and he nodded, possibly in brief acceptance of her apology, though she had the suspicion he had no intention of making it easy for her.

'If you want me to get out, please stop the cab,' she offered, desperately hoping he'd do so. Her nerves would be threadbare if she had to travel far in his company.

However, her hopes were soon shattered when he shrugged carelessly.

'You're here, now so you may as well stay. I'm going into town, so I hope that suits you, seeing as you've now decided to join me.'

The irony was unmistakable but Mickey chose to ignore it, striving to keep her voice level as she answered. 'Well, I was hoping you could drop me off at Chiswick, actually, I'm anxious to get home just as soon as I can.'

'So I gathered,' he said coldly, 'but I'm afraid it's out of the question. I'm going straight into town.'

'Oh, but it's only a short detour, couldn't you . . .'

'No, I couldn't,' he said, cutting her off abruptly. Mickey turned away in dismay. Her original plan had been to persuade the occupant of the taxi to drop her off first, then continue his journey, but she knew it would be just wasting her breath trying to pursue it. She had the strongest feeling he would enjoy repeating his refusal, just to even their score. No, now she would have to content herself with travelling into the city with him, then commandeer the taxi after he got out. She bit back a weary sigh of annoyance. So far her wonderful special tactics had only added more time rather than less to her journey. Why did she always have to be so impulsive, never think things through? Still, it was her own fault, from start to finish, so she'd just have to make the best of it.

Settling back against the slippery leather seat, she pushed her glasses more firmly up the smooth, straight little slope of her nose and looked out of the window, the sweeping brim of her hat hiding her face from his view.

She was incredibly conscious of him sitting next to her, terribly aware of even the slightest movement of his big, muscled body, and she fought to dismiss him from her mind by fixing her attention on the passing scene.

Dusk had dropped completely now and the cars were all lit, their headlamps making a golden procession along the busy highway. Dimly seen landmarks unfolded along the route, and slowly Mickey felt the comfort of sheer familiarity sweep through her, easing her tension.

It was so good to be back. She had enjoyed her trip, enjoyed the fast pace of life in the USA, enjoyed the challenge of working with new people in a new environment, but a month had been long enough.

True, she had been pleased that her work had been greeted with such enthusiasm, had been flattered to be offered a longer, permanent contract, but not enough so to make her accept. Although the salary mentioned had been a staggering increase on what she now earned, and was obviously a great temptation, it had not been enough of an inducement to make her uproot her whole life and move there permanently. No . . . this was her home town and she loved it.

'Did you enjoy your holiday? Which part of America did you see?' The rich voice cut through her musings and she jumped slightly, turning to glance in his direction, looking for any ulterior motive to his question. There seemed to be nothing other that courteous interest in his expression, so she accepted it at face value; anything would be better than a strained silence for the next twenty minutes or so until they reached town.

'Philadelphia,' she answered politely, shifting slightly so that she faced him. 'It wasn't all holiday, actually. I was working, too.'

'Oh?'

There was note of enquiry in his voice which it would have been churlish to ignore, so she elaborated.

'Yes. I was working on one of the early morning news programmes . . .'

'So that's it, you're a reporter!'

Cold accusation ringed his voice and he swivelled to face her, one large hand shooting out to grasp her forearm in a steely grip. With a yelp of fright Mickey tugged at his restraining hold, automatically twisting her arm sharply downwards, instantly breaking his grasp. Quickly she drew back into the corner, nursing her tender flesh. A flicker of pleasure raced through her at his look of pure astonishment . . . if he thought he could start the heavy stuff with her he'd be in for a shock!

'Where the hell did you learn a trick like that?' he ground out, staring down at his empty hand before running his eyes over her slender five-foot-three-inch frame as though searching for hidden muscles.

'Oh, here and there, but be warned, it's not only one I know, so keep your hands to yourself.'

She managed to keep the smugness from her tone . . . just. Years of self-defence classes had finally paid off, and it had been worth every bruised inch just to see the expression on his face. It was invigorating to know that her skills actually did work in a practical situation!

'Lady, I wouldn't touch you again with a barge-pole,' he retorted with feeling and some of her smugness vanished. Surely she didn't look that awful?

Swiftly her eyes shot past him to the darkend mirror-like surface of the taxi window, and she swallowed a grimace, wryly acknowledging she was a mess. Why on earth hadn't she allowed herself more time before she was due at the airport, fixed up her face and hair? She could have done with the extra boost to her confidence right at this moment. Still, no point worrying now, there was little she could do about it.

'Which paper do you work for?'

The harsh question cut through her self-absorbed study, and she flicked her glance back towards him, a shiver of alarm trickling through her. There was a dangerous stillness to his hard features, a burning anger deep in the blue eyes which gleamed even through the dim-shadowed interior of the cab, and she eyed him warily, quickly trying to assess the situation.

He hadn't been delighted when she had leapt into the taxi, but he had definitely not been this hostile. Just what had upset him so much that he looked ready to commit murder? Swiftly she ran back over their brief and disastrous acquaintanceship, and suddenly it hit her. He had caught her reading his notes on the plane and now believed, quite wrongly, that she was a reporter; two facts which added up to one big mess.

Opening her mouth, she was about to reassure him that he had nothing to worry about, that she was not in a position to spill his darkest secrets to the world, when he demanded harshly, 'Well, answer me, then.'

It was an order, no more, no less, and if there was one thing Mickey couldn't stand it was taking orders. Looking down, she hastily hid the flare of annoyance which crossed her face. Just who did he think he was telling her what to do? All idea of reassuring him fled instantly, to be replaced by a feeling of quite malicious intent. He'd made the mistake, now let him suffer. He deserved to.

Raising her head, she met his gaze levelly.

'The *Recorder*.' Her tone was coolly neutral, exposing none of her true feelings.

'The *Recorder*—that's a national, isn't it?'

'Yes. With one of the top readerships in the country.' Oh, it was blissful to rub it in, like salt, and watch him squirm.

A rapid play of emotions crossed his deeply tanned face and she watched carefully, appreciating his dilemma and interested to see the outcome. Would he refer to her earlier probing, ask her not to reveal anything she'd read, or would he choose to ignore it and thus hope not to precipitate matters? It was a tricky decision which needed careful balancing, needed time. She'd give him a few minutes.

Quietly she settled back deep into her corner, studying him thoughtfully. Just who was he, if he thought people would be interested in his exploits? Her eyes ran over the carved planes of his face, seeking something familiar in the curve of cheek and brow, but she could find nothing. She didn't recognise him, but obviously others would; she'd have to make some enquiries. Her interest was definitely aroused now. What was his name, though?

Quickly she delved back into her memory, sieving the information through to pick out the few facts she knew . . . Grant. That was it, the hostess had called him Mr Grant, and if she remembered correctly he had the initials KG on his case.

Right, Mr K Grant, she thought, I don't know who you are yet, but by heaven, I'm not going to let you know that.

Turning towards him, she pinned a gentle little smile to the soft fullness of her lips. Let him sweat!

The minutes ticked slowly on and Mickey felt her jaw begin to stiffen under the strain of holding the smile. Surely he wasn't going to give her the silent treatment all the way into town? That seemed quite out of character. Suddenly he looked up, a smile of such devastating charm and brilliance crossing his face that she blinked in the glare from it. Dazzled, she smiled back, rather more warmly than she intended to.

'I don't suppose it would be any use appealing to your better instincts,' he murmured huskily, his eyes holding hers, and she gulped, swallowing audibly.

The dark-brown voice was back with a vengeance, running like hot treacle through her veins, and she fought to control her melting bloodstream. Taking a deep breath, she closed her hazel eyes, turning briefly away. Her pulse was popping like champagne bubbles and she pressed a finger to her wrist, trying to stem the eruption. Her instincts were aroused, all right, though she doubted if they could be classed as 'better' ones. Desperately, she tried to get the wild clamour ringing through her under control, remember her desire to make him suffer which had seemed so strong only minutes before, but was now disappearing at a rapid pace. She had to be sensible, think clearly. But it was no good; at this moment she'd agree to anything just to receive another of those thousand volt smiles.

Turning swiftly back, she opened her mouth to assure him of her compliance when her eyes caught a fleeting but oh-so-clear expression on his face and she stopped.

He'd done it deliberately; he'd turned on the neon-bright charm, switched on the magical voice, knowing exactly what sort of effect they would have on a poor susceptible female. And she'd nearly fallen for it. Why, of all the sneaky, low-down, double-dealing rats, he had to be king! Thank heavens she'd sussed him out before she'd made a complete fool of herself! But she'd show him. Two could play at that little game . . . she'd make queen rat yet!

Leaning forwards slightly, she rested one slim, pale little hand softly against the cord-covered hardness of his arm, staring limpidly up into his blue eyes, her full lips curved into an adoring and appreciative smile.

Swiftly he covered her slim fingers with his own, squeezing them gently, staring down into her upturned face, smiling.

'Well? The word dropped as softly as a puff of thistledown into the silence.

'No,' she murmured sweetly.

For a brief second his smile held, before rapidly melting away under the heat of his fury.

'No! What do you mean, *no*?'

Brusquely, he swatted her hand from his arm, turning to stare belligerently at her. In the dim, flickering glow from the passing street-lamps, his face was set, a rugged terrain of planes and shadows, and she drew well back before elaborating further.

'I mean, no, it wouldn't be any use appealing to my better instincts,' she stated, clearly and slowly, as though addressing a slightly backward child.

The words sank rapidly into the quicksand of his charm, transforming it into threatening temper. For an instant, a mere flicker of time, his hand lifted from his knee, the fingers clenching convulsively into a throat-sized curl, and instinctively Mickey grasped the strap of her heavy bag. It was blatantly obvious that he wasn't used to being crossed, and she wouldn't hesitate to use it if he turned nasty. Hit now, think later, had been one maxim which had stood her in good stead over the years, and she was not about to relinquish it now.

With a supreme effort of will he got himself under control, though whether through gentlemanly instinct or just plain old-fashioned caution, remembering his last assault on her, it was hard to decide. She wasted no time in worrying. She might have won the first coup, but the battle was far from over. She'd need all her reserves for his next attack, and it wasn't long in coming.

Turning to face her, he ran cold eyes over her slight figure; instinctively she sat up a touch straighter, a tinge of colour edging the soft curve of her cheek. A hint of a smile stirred his mouth, showing as the briefest flash of white teeth between the trimmed edges of his luxuriant beard as he noticed her action, and she silently berated herself for allowing him to score even a small point. Quickly, she got herself under control, raising a quizzical eyebrow in his direction, waiting for him to speak.

'Well, as it appears I can't appeal to your better instincts, how about your worst?' he grated out.

Slipping a hand inside the loose folds of his jacket, he drew out a thick leather wallet, flipping it open to run his fingers over the crisp sheaf of notes wedged inside. He cast her a brief glance, his eyes devoid of any colour in the dim interior of the cab, gleaming like flat, cold coins.

'How much?'

'I beg your pardon?' Horrified, Mickey stared back at him, scarcely able to believe what she had heard. Was he really offering her money, hoping to buy her silence, her compliance?

'You heard me. How much do you want to keep what you've seen to yourself?'

Carelessly he dragged a fistful of notes from the brown leather, bending them in half to run the ball of his thumb assessingly across their crackling edges.

'I guess there must be a couple of thousand pounds

here,' he stated flatly, raising his eyes to run them insultingly over the full length of her body. 'I would imagine you could buy yourself quite a few decent things with that, wouldn't you?'

Deliberately, he held the wad of notes towards her, and with a small gasp Micky recoiled in horror, more insulted than she'd ever been in her life. How dared he, how dared he offer to buy her off, and even worse, how dared he imply that she looked as though she was in desperate need of the money? It was the final straw!

Turning, she rapped sharply on the glass screen which separated them from the driver.

'Stop the taxi,' she ordered, anger adding volume to her normally quiet voice.

With a screech the vehicle ground to a halt, the driver turning round towards her, ready to object to the tone of her order. However, one quick look at her fury-contorted face soon changed his mind, and he rapidly changed his mind. He'd had enough experience of lovers' quarrels to know when not to buttin. Let them sort it out between them, he wasn't going to step into the firing line.

The abruptness of their halt had dislodged the huge tote-bag from Mickey's lap, spilling its contents all over the back of the cab. Muttering wildly, she began snatching up her things, stuffing them haphazardly back with scant regard for order. The man sat quietly watching her, his eyes following her frantic movements, making no attempt to help. It was difficult to see in the half-light, but she thought she had everything, unless there was something left on the floor. Quicky she ran her foot over the few inches of space next to her suitcase, swearing softly, with a sad lack of ladylike control, when she felt the shaft of her favourite pen snap under the crushing pressure of her boot heel. Bending awkwardly sideways, she picked it up, feeling the clinging stickiness of spilt ink stain her fingers. One-handed, she scrabbled in her coat pocket for a tissue, finding nothing but an empty crisp packet, but it would

have to do. She carefully dropped the leaking pen
inside, twisting the top tight to keep the rest of the ink
from spilling out, before pushing it right to the bottom
of her bag. Her fingers still gleamed wetly in the dim
light, and she looked round for something to dry them
on.

'Here.'

A crumpled but clean white handkerchief was thrust
towards her, but she hestiated, loath to accept anything
from him. With a murmur of disgust he tossed it on to
her lap before turning to stare out of the window.

Picking it up, Mickey fastidiously wiped every finger
on its clean folds, deliberately rubbing the stain into the
soft linen, as she would have enjoyed rubbing his face
into something not so pleasant. It helped work off
some, but only some, of her outrage. With every finger
dry, though now coloured a delicate if indistinct shade
of violet, she looked up abruptly, meeting his gaze, and
had the strongest feeling that he knew exactly what
she'd been thinking. Heat flooded her cheeks and she
dropped her eyes, making a great show of refolding the
marbled linen into a perfect square before silently
offering it back to him.

He accepted it with a mockingly courteous smile,
stuffing it back into the pocket of his trousers. The
wallet still lay on his knee, the loose notes fanned over
its soft, buffed-leather surface, and her eyes were
unwillingly drawn towards it.

Following her gaze he picked it up, flicking carelessly
at the wad of money.

'Do I take it the answer's no yet again, then?' he
questioned lightly, as easily as though he had been
offering her a cup of tea, a biscuit, anything but two
thousand pounds. Quickly her eyes recoiled.

'I don't think I really need to answer that, do I?' she
replied tartly. 'You can take your money, Mr Grant,
and I'm quite sure that you know exactly just what you
can do with it!'

Grasping the door-handle, she swung it open, sliding

herself out into the cool, fresh chill of the night air before bending to grip the handle of her suitcase. Awkwardly she eased it back towards the gaping doorway, pausing with it balanced on the sill, her eyes running scornfully over the tall, silent figure.

'Goodnight, Mr Grant. I'd be lying if I said it had been a pleasurable meeting, for either one of us, but at least you've had the opportunity to learn one thing tonight. Neither I nor my silence are for sale, not now, not ever.' Her voice rang clear in the night's stillness, and she felt quite pleased with the noble effect of her words.

Bending forwards, he stared back at her, his shadowed face moving briefly into the clear lights of a passing car. Contempt, cynicism, experience, all shone in the frosted depths of his glittering eyes, shivered through the iron-hard tone of his deep voice.

'Don't kid yourself, lady. There's not a woman born who can't be bought. It's just a matter of finding your price, that's all.' Reaching over, he shoved her case off its precarious perch with a disdainful hand, snapping the door closed, missing her fingers by inches. Then with a roar the taxi pulled away, leaving her standing in a dim yellow pool of lamplight, staring after it, gasping with frustrated outrage.

It was a bitter thing to admit, but she had the nasty suspicion she hadn't won that round, after all!

CHAPTER TWO

THE MORNING was still, quiet, the sound of traffic muted at this early hour when most people were still sleeping, and lying in bed, Mickey desperately wished she could join them. She'd been awake for hours now, ever since the first pale, thin rays of sunlight had filtered through the curtains, and her head ached with a throbbing tiredness. Closing her eyes, she tried to will herself back to sleep, but it was useless. Her mind was just too busy, too full of a jumbling whirl of images to let her rest, and with a sigh she slithered up into a sitting position, yelping sharply as the blistered edge of her sore heel caught against a fold in the sheet.

Pushing the covers aside, she eased her leg up, bringing the injured foot into closer view, and ran a gentle, tentative finger over the red, inflamed skin . . . wincing. The blister was huge, completely covering the back of her heel; it would be days before she'd be able to stand any pressure on it, before she'd even be able to wear a shoe, and it was all that wretched man's fault! Leaning back against the soft, padded headboard, Mickey let her mind drift back over the previous disastrous evening.

After she'd jumped from the cab in such a fury of self-righteous indignation it had taken several minutes before she'd realised she was virtually stranded. True, there were taxis passing, but all of them were full and none responded to her urgent signals. Her only hope lay in catching a bus and, gathering up her case and bag, Mickey had headed off towards the nearest bus stop.

By the time she'd reached it her arms were trembling with the strain of carrying her luggage, and it was with relief that she'd set it down and opened her bag to find some money for the fare . . . and that was when she had

22

found she really was in trouble!

No amount of searching could unearth her purse, and finally she'd been forced to accept the fact that she must have dropped it when her bag had spilled open in the taxi. Desperate to find some money, she'd scrabbled quickly through her pockets, and finally come up with the princely sum of one dollar and fifty cents. It was a fair enough amount, granted, but not one she felt acceptable to London Transport, and with a sigh she had been forced to face the fact that if she intended to get home that evening it would have to be by the most basic and cheapest method possible . . . Shank's pony!

Thirty-five minutes it had taken her, thirty-five miserable minutes of struggling, so that when she had finally made it she'd been too exhausted to feel anything other than mild relief. Now, however, lying in bed, her foot bearing the unmistakable evidence of her labours, it was a rather different story, and anger started to curl inside her as she faced the unpalatable fact that she'd been insulted, near-assaulted and then abandoned, but had no clear idea why. Oh, granted, she could understand the man being a trifle annoyed at what she'd done, but surely there was little justification for his subsequent actions? Just who was he? Why were those score sheets so important to him that he was willing to try first seduction, then later bribery, to safegurad them?

It was a puzzle, which had kept her tossing and turning right through the night, but Mickey knew she was still no closer to solving it. There were just too many pieces missing, too many unexplained details. With a murmur of annoyance she gave up trying and climbed out of bed. To hell with him and all his problems; she had quite enough of her own to attend to.

Crossing the room, she snatched her old robe from the hook behind the door and slipped her feet into a pair of backless mules, then scuffed down the stairs, the loose footwear clattering horribly on the bare wooden boards, making her head ache harder than ever. Tears of tiredness and self-pity welled in her eyes, and she sat down abruptly on one splintery tread, nursing her throbbing temples. Just what had she done to deserve all this?

The answer came to her, swift and simple—snooping—and she was forced to admit it might be right. Every since she had snooped, read that insufferable man's papers, things had gone from bad to worse. It must be some form of retribution. If only she'd had the sense to control her curiosity and impulsiveness in the first place, then probably none of the events last night would have happened, and she'd be feeling better able to cope with this other mess.

Standing, she gazed around, grateful that she'd forgotten to put her glasses on so could only half see the chaos left in the small hallway; quite frankly, she doubted if she was up to the full effect just at the moment. Despairingly, she took short-sighted stock of her surroundings.

The walls had been scraped bare of paper, huge, gaping cracks in the crumbling grey plaster now being their only adornment. A thick film of grit lay over every surface, nestling in the carvings on the banister rail, crunching under her slippered feet. Carbuncles of solidified plaster erupted from the parquet floor, its once gleaming surface now dull and scratched. A small mountain of used sandwich wrappings and empty cans lay in one corner, which had evidently been designated the rubbish dump. In fact, except for the pristine fresh pile of unused dust sheets stacked on the bend of the stairs, everywhere and everything was a mess, and when she got her hands on the builder she'd kill him!

A simple job, he'd assured her, just a week's work and the whole hallway would be transformed. Well, it was transformed all right, but not in the way she had expected, and fury surged through her. If he had any sense he would never darken her doorstep again . . . It would take her days to clear up this mess.

Grabbing up the trailing skirts of the old, worn robe,

she strode down the rest of the stairs, pausing at the bottom to wipe the grey film from her fingers and cast a despairing look round. Just where should she start?

The doorbell rang, echoing loudly round the near-empty hallway and she jumped, putting a steadying hand to her throat to calm her leaping pulse. Who on earth could it be? No one knew she was due back yet apart from Rob . . . surely he wouldn't be calling so early, would he?

The thought disturbed her, made her hesitate before she answered the shrill summons. She'd known Rob Bryant for several years now, ever since she'd first started writing for the paper where he was one of the top photographers, and gradually over this time had built up a warm and easy friendship with him. Just recently, though, Mickey had gained the distinct impression that Rob was looking for something more than just friendship from the relationship; something she wasn't certain she could give him. Oh, she was fond of Rob, very fond, and enjoyed the warm, comfortable hours they spent together, but deep inside she knew there was just that tiny but important 'something' missing. Not that she expected lights flashing and bells ringing when she did fall in love, she was far too sensible and level-headed for that, but surely there would be something . . . even if it was only a tiny tingle. No, she loved Rob but wasn't in love with him, that was the difference. The trouble was, how on earth could she tell him? There was no way she wanted to hurt his feelings, but equally there was no way she wanted him to keep on hoping for something which might never be. It was a problem, and one she didn't feel up to handling right at the moment!

The bell rang again, longer, louder, as though the caller was leaning an elbow on the button, and suddenly Mickey knew with absolute certainty that it wouldn't be Rob. There was no way mild, gentle-mannered Rob would ring so agressively, so who could it be . . . unless it was the builder come back to sort out his mess. Oh, just let her get at him!

With a warlike gleam in her hazel eyes she leapt forwards, pushing the tangle of black curls from her face. Dragging the door open, she flung it back, setting it bouncing on straining hinges.

'You louse, you worm, you . . . *you*?'

Horrified, she stared up at the tall, bearded figure lounging against her door-jamb, one eyebrow raised in mocking surprise. Straightening, he ran an insolently lazy glance over her dishevelled figure, and Mickey felt the blood rush pell-mell to her cheeks as she realised just what she must look like with her sleep-creased face and tangled hair, not to mention the old robe. Despite the fact that he was quite the last person she'd either expected or hoped to see at her door, she was vain enough to mind him finding her like this, and annoyance sparked through her like a firecracker.

'What do you want?' she demanded with a sad lack of grace, clutching the gaping neckline of the robe closed.

'Tut, tut, Miss James, is this an example of all that British hospitality I've heard so much about? he asked mockingly.

Dressed in slim-fitting black cords and jacket, offset by a deep blue knit shirt, and with the sunlight fairly bouncing off his thick, streaked hair, he looked so stunningly masculine and vital that she could have wept with sheer frustration. Why couldn't she have been dressed, been looking good? Next to him, she felt like some unkempt slug which had just crawled from under a rather large stone. It just wasn't fair. However, there was no way she was going to bow down before her obvious shortcomings, and she rounded on him snappily.

'Hospitality? I wouldn't show you any hospitality if we were the last two people left on a desert island and I had the last coconut, Mr Grant. Now, as I said before, what do you want? I've a lot to do.'

'Obviously,' he replied, looking over her shoulder at the chaos behind. Mickey could have kicked herself for drawing his attention to it. Moving fractionally, she

she edged the door over, hoping that at least the unlicensed refuse tip would pass unnoticed. She opened her mouth to explain the mess, but snapped it shut quickly before any words could escape. What business was it of his what her house was like? Dumbly she stared back at him, waiting for the explanation for his visit, and he treated her to another of his smug little smiles.

'Well, as it appears I'm not going to get invited in, I'd better say my piece here on the step. I believe I have something you may be interested in.'

Sliding his hand inside his jacket pocket, he started to draw something out when Mickey reached forward and grasped his arm, trying to suck in enough breath to give full vent to her outrage which, after all she had suffered last night, had magnified tenfold. Like a mini eruption, the words roared from her lips.

'How dare you, how dare you come here and offer me money after last night? I've told you before and I'll tell you again, here and now, for the very last time: There is no way, absolutely no way you can buy me, Mr Grant. I'm not for sale!'

The words rang out, echoing across the morning's stillness, and even Mickey was surprised by their sheer volume. Several startled birds flew from the holly bush, and she swung her eyes towards the sudden flurry of movement, almost choking with horror as she caught sight of the two women pausing by the gate. From the looks on their faces they must heard every single word, and she shuddered to think what sort of interpretation they had placed on them. A deep, embarrassed flush stained her cheeks and she leant weakly back against the sun-warmed wood of the door, her eyes closed. How would she ever be able to go into the high street again, ever face them?

The soft, low sound of a chuckle cut through her misery and, opening her eyes, she stared at the tall figure propped against the house wall, tears of mirth sparkling in his blue eyes.

'Why, you . . .' Incensed that he, the cause of her

problems, should be deriving so much enjoyment from her discomfiture, Mickey swung a small fist towards him, aiming for that laughing face.

It never connected. With lightning speed a large, tanned hand shot out, catching her slender wrist and holding it fast. Beyond caution, she raised her other hand, aiming for the same target but that, too, was quickly trapped. With a gallingly effortless ease he pushed her arms down, crossing them low behind her back and forcing her close against his hard frame with a jolt which sent the air from her lungs.

'No one, but no one, takes a swing at me, lady, and gets away with it,' he ground out.

For one brief second he glared down into her startled face, his eyes like burning ice. Then with a swift, inescapable movement he lowered his head, taking her lips in a hard and savage kiss which tingled through to her very core. He rolled his mouth roughly over hers, forcing her lips apart, thrusting his tongue into her deep, dark sweetness, and Mickey, crushed against the unyielding hardness of his big body, was powerless to resist.

Tears of impotent fury sparkled in her eyes as she desperately tried to turn her head away from his merciless kiss, but it was useless. Grasping both her slender wrists in one hand, he clamped the other at the back of her head and held her still.

The kiss ran on and on, and slowly she became aware of a change, a lessening of the savagery. Now his lips and tongue had another aim rather than just punishment: nibbling, tasting, tantalising, they demanded a response. For a few seconds she fought against the hot tide of feeling which was swirling through her, clinging desperately to her anger to fuel her resistance, but it was hopeless; sensation washed through her till she felt boneless, mindless, every fibre reacting to his touch.

With a low, defeated groan she kissed him back, pressing herself closer against the solid muscles of his chest. Fire licked along her veins, burned under her skin as he moved his mouth slowly from hers to trail a scattering of nibbling kisses from the corner of her lips to the vulnerable hollow below her ear and she shuddered uncontrollably.

For one long moment more he held her against him, before slowly he set her away and glanced out towards the garden, a strange stillness to his face. Then, lowering his head, he flicked her a brief glance, his eyes not quite meeting hers as he said softly, 'I think I'd better come in, don't you?' His voice was deep, slightly husky, and Mickey nodded, unable to find the strength to speak.

Stepping round him, she gently closed the door, pausing for an instant, her hand pressed against the cool metal clasp of the lock. She felt stunned, surprised, shocked by the intensity of her reaction to him . . . a stranger. Swinging round, she studied the broad back turned towards her, her ears catching the faint but unmistakable sound of his ragged breathing, and a faint glimmer of triumph shimmered through her.

Hard and tough though he may be, Mr K Grant was far from unmoved by their little encounter. Maybe, just maybe, she'd hit him with something even more powerful than the punch she intended!

Head high, back rigid, sagging hem trailing in the dust, Mickey led the way along the hall to the kitchen, and after a moment's hesitation he followed.

Pushing open the door, she blinked at the sudden flood of sunlight which dazzled her eyes, stopping abruptly as her vision swam with a myriad of coloured dots. Unprepared for her sudden halt, he cannoned into the back of her and she winced as the toe of his shoe caught her sore heel.

'Sorry.' Swiftly he steadied her, his large hands gripping the tops of her arms just fractionally longer than was perhaps nesessary.

A sudden rush of awareness flooded through her, and hastily she stepped away, crossing the room to set the width of the table between them. She was far too sensitive at the moment, too aware, to feel safe so close to him.

'Please sit down, Mr Grant,' she offered formally, forcing a coolly polite tone to her voice. 'I'll make us a drink, though I'm afraid it will have to be tea, as I don't drink coffee.'

'Thank you, tea will be fine.'

He matched her tone and for an instant she eyed him warily. Even with what little she knew, it seemed out of character for him to be so amenable. Still, there was nothing in the hard mask of his face which gave her any clue to his real feelings and, turning away, she filled the kettle and plugged it in, glad to have some small task to occupy her shaking hands. She could feel his eyes following her as she moved round the kitchen, collecting two of the red, patterned mugs and a small jug of milk from the fridge, but she avoided his gaze, knowing she had to hold on to her composure.

Within minutes she had the tea made and poured and, sitting herself down at the table, she took a small sip of the hot liquid, needing something to revive her. Looking up, she stared levelly at him, her voice firm as she said clearly, 'Right then, Mr Grant, let's have it . . . the reason why you're here.'

Watching her face, he reached inside his jacket, raising a peremptory hand to forestall the words he could see forming on her lips. Smoothly he drew out a square of red leather, placing it gently in the exact centre of the table, saying nothing. For a few stunned seconds Mickey stared, before reaching out and snatching it up. Quickly she flipped the purse open, needing to see her name inside, even though she knew it was hers. Looking up, she stared into his unreadable blue eyes.

'It's my purse. Where did you get it?'

He smiled thinly back at her, a faintly mocking curve to his chiselled mouth.

'I found it last night,' he replied easily, 'as you were getting out of the cab.' He watched her face calmly, waiting for her reaction.

For a second she was slow to catch on, then suddenly the true meaning of his words slammed through her brain.

'You found it *as* I was getting out? You mean you knew it was there and you let me go without it?'

'Yes.'

'Why, you . . .'

Words failed her; there just weren't enough nasty names in her vocabulary to deal with a man like this, though she had the strongest suspicion she might be inventing a few new ones pretty soon. Gulping in a swift breath of air, she fought to speak, stumbling till righteous indignation sent the words tumbling from her lips like a waterfall.

'Do you realise just what I went through last night because you'd seen fit to keep my purse? Do you? No? Well, let me tell you. I had to walk home—d'you hear me?—walk for over thirty minutes, lugging that suitcase with me while I fielded offers of lifts from 'gentlemen' who had something other than being Good Samaritans on their minds. Then, when I did finally get here, I had to phone the office and was greeted by a whole bagful of complaints because I was so late filing my copy. And, as if that wasn't enough for one evening, I ended up with this for my efforts.'

Lifting up her trailing skirts, she shot one dainty size three foot out for his inspection, turning it so he could better appreciate the blister in all its glory. Anger rippled through her; if she had blamed his unreasonable behaviour last night for her injury, then she blamed his subsequent actions even more.

'Mmmm, nasty, though the rest of it looks in good shape,' he murmured, running an assessing eye up the slender length of her leg. She blushed, hastily dropping her hemline and rounding on him angrily.

'Is that all you can say, then?'

'Well, Miss James, I don't see how you can reasonably blame me for your unfortunate choice of footwear, can you?' he replied easily tilting the chair to rest on its back legs.

For a split second Mickey had the insane desire to give him a sharp push and enjoy seeing the smug smile leave his face, before she hastily squashed it down. It could be asking for rather more trouble than she could handle right at this moment. Rubbing a weary hand across her aching forhead, she drew in a deep breath, trying to think rationally. Why on earth had he done it? There must be a reason. Why should he keep her purse and then go to the trouble of bringing it back? It just didn't make sense. Dropping her hands, she gave him a puzzled look.

'Why?' she questioned. 'Why did you do it?'

For a brief moment he studied her puzzled face, his face betraying nothing. When he spoke, the harsh edge to his voice made her flinch. 'Quite frankly, Miss James, it was too good an opportunity to miss. There were certain facts I needed to find out about you and this seemed the ideal way.'

'What facts?' she shot back at him, astounded.

'Your name, for one thing. Don't forget you had the advantage over me—you knew who I was, but I hadn't any idea who you were, other than the fact you worked for the 'Recorder'. I needed to know a lot more about you than that, find some way that I could guarantee that you wouldn't print what you'd read.'

With a helpless shrug, Mickey gazed back at him. 'I'm afraid I just don't understand what you mean. There's no guarantee that I can give you, other than my word, and of course, you have that. I have no intention of divulging anything I saw, Mr Grant, neither to the paper nor to anyone else.'

For a brief moment she toyed with the idea of explaining just what she did at the paper; perhaps that would reassure him, but there again she doubted it. He didn't seem the type of man who would change his mind easily, and the very fact she was employed by the paper would weigh heavily against her. Quite frankly, she was at a loss to know just what he wanted from her, what he

expected, apart maybe from a pact signed in blood . . .
would that convince him?

'And just how do I know that you'll keep your
word?' he demanded roughly. 'You had very few
scruples in reading my papers in the first place, so I'm
afraid I can set little store by your word. No, Miss
James, what I'm looking for is something much more
solid and permanent than your word, a proper business
contract, in fact, which will not only set my mind at
ease, but will put several thousand pounds at your
disposal. So what do you say?'

There was only one word she could think of, only one
quite matched the occasion, and with a gloriously
dramatic gesture she stood up and, pointing towards the
door, said it.

'Out!'

Unmoved by her obvious displeasure, he swallowed
the rest of his tea before standing and sliding the chair
neatly back into place. Resting his hand on its slatted
back, he ran a lazy glance over her quivering figure.

'It's a pity, you know. We could have come to a very
satisfactory arrangement over this; you could have had
several thousand pounds to play about with, and I'd
have had the security of knowing we had a proper deal.
Now, well, now it probably won't come to such a
pleasant conclusion. Are you quite sure you don't want
to reconsider? It's your last chance.'

'Out,' she repeated, too incensed to hear the note of
warning underlying his deep voice. 'I've had all I can
take from you, Mr Grant, with your offers and insults,
absolutely all. Now, get out!' Whirling, she snatched up
her half-empty mug, balancing it as though preparing to
bowl at his head.

Raising his hands in mock surrender, he strode
unhurriedly from the room, and with a shudder Mickey
set the dripping cup back on the table before hurrying
after him. Opening the front door, she stood to one side
to let him pass, carefully averting her eyes from his
mocking face.

'Well, if you're quite sure you won't reconsider . . .' He paused fractionally, so close that she could feel the heat from his body pass through the thin folds of her robe, and she turned her head, a steely determination in her hazel eyes.

'Never,' she said briefly, her voice laced with scorn.

'Pity.'

For one brief second he held her gaze, a strange, fleeting hint of regret in his azure eyes which puzzled her. Then suddenly he caught hold of her shoulders and dragged her towards him, and for one startled instant she froze, before coming swiftly back to her senses. Flinging her arms upwards she tried to break his hold and regain her freedom, but he knew all the moves, anticipating her reaction by changing his grip and pinning both her arms back down at her sides. Undaunted, she tried again, shooting her leg forwards to hook it round the back of his and pull him off balance. The blistered sore on her heel caught on the rough fabric of his trousers, and she flinched with pain, instantly losing momentum.

'Naughty, naughty,' he murmured, a faint flush of triumph rimming his hard cheekbones.

With a relentless strength he pressed her back against the door, using his long, hard body to trap her, to make it impossible for her to try any more of her well-rehearsed throws. Then, dipping his head, he préssed his lips to hers in a hard yet strangely impersonal kiss which held none of the anger nor the passion of the previous one.

For a brief moment more she struggled, trying to twist her head away, but stopping abruptly as several bright flashes filled her vision. My heaven, he kissed her and she saw stars!

'Did you get that one, too, Ted?'

The low question rumbled from the lips now hovering close to her ear, and she jumped, instinctively looking towards the front garden.

'Sure did, Keir. Probably won't be as good as the

earlier ones . . . the light was better then, but it should
do. I'll let you have the prints in about an hour.'

Confusion ran fast through her brain; just who was
that man in her garden, and what was he doing with that
camera? In startled enquiry she swung her gaze up
towards the tall, bearded figure looming over her, and
he smiled grimly back, a faint, malicious sparkle to the
blue eyes.

'Not worked it out yet, Miss James? Come now, I'd
have thought you'd have known all the angles in your
game,' he said nastily, putting a pace between them
before rubbing the palms of his hands down the side
seams of his trousers, as though he'd just been in
contact with something nasty. He shot her another brief
glance as she still stood silently watching him.

'Still not got it, I see. Well, let me explain. My friend
has just taken several very nice photographs of us this
morning, sharing what to outsiders would appear to be
some very passionate embraces. The fact that you are
still in your nightclothes only adds a touch more interest
to them, of course. Now, Miss James, it's really quite
simple: if you breathe one word, just one, to your
paper, I'll see that copies of those photographs, plus an
interesting if imaginative account of our relationship,
are sent to one of more salacious Sunday papers. After
that, who's going to believe a word you say? After all,
what's that saying about a woman scorned, Miss
James? And that's just how you will appear . . . I shall
make absolutely certain of it.'

She stared at him helplessly, unable to believe what
she was hearing. Surely he wouldn't, couldn't . . . Why,
it was . . .

'Blackmail,' he assured her, raising a deceptively
gentle finger to lift her drooping jaw back into place.
'Blackmail, pure and simple, but very, very effective.'

Turning, he walked unhurriedly to the car parked at
the end of her pathway, and drove away without a
backward glance.

With a muttered oath, Mickey slammed the door,

then raced back down the hall, dodging the piles of
rubbish with all the skill of a champion hurdler.
Entering the kitchen, she snatched up the now-tainted
mug he'd used and hurled it at the tiled wall, wishing
she'd given in to the urge before and had the pleasure of
seeing it splinter against his head! Bending, she picked
up the other mug and prepared to bowl, when a small
voice of reason surfaced through her fury. The mugs
had been expensive and, through accident and now
design, she was down to the last three; it was just stupid
to waste another on that man . . . He wasn't worth it!

Carefully, delicately, she set it back on the table, her
eyes tracing the swirling pattern as though it might offer
some answer to the maze of questions filling her head.

Why had he done it? Why on earth had he gone to
such lengths to ensure her silence, and why had he
chosen such an incredible way? She couldn't understand
it. Pulling out a chair, she sat slowly down, resting the
softly rounded curve of her chin on the heel of her hand,
while she tried to think. Quickly her mind raced back
over the sheaf of papers she'd read on the plane and she
briefly recalled some of the scores and comments,
though she would be hard pushed to relate the correct
name to the correct total. She might make some
headway if she knew just what he'd written them for,
but she didn't. In fact, come to that, she didn't really
know who he was, but she was going to find out!

She crossed the room to the phone and dialled
quickly, asking to be put through to Alistair Graham
when the receptionist answered. If anyone would know
who he was, it would be Alistair; he edited the paper's
gossip page, and sometimes Mickey had the feeling
there wasn't a single person left in the whole world
whom he didn't know something about.

The low, lazy voice answered and quickly Mickey set
her mind to the task. Alistair might give the impression
of being a slow-moving tortoise, but it was all a blind;
he had a razor-sharp mind and a fine-honed instinct for
smelling out a story. She'd have to tread very carefully

if she didn't want to awaken his interest too much, and quite frankly, given this morning's little episode, she just couldn't afford to!

'Alistair . . . Mickey James here. How are you?' She kept her voice pleasant and casual, allowing no hint of the raging sea of questions to tinge its tone.

'Mickey, love, when did you get back?'

'Last night, around eight-thirty.'

'Good. Now, what can I do for you?'

There was a touch of curiosity to his slow voice and she rapidly rehearsed what she was going to say before taking a deep, breath.

'Well, I was just being nosey actually, Alistair. There was a man on the plane last night, in fact I was seated next to him, and I just wondered if you had any idea who he might be. I had the feeling he might be someone you'd heard of.'

Did it sound likely? Would he accept the enquiry at face value, or would he delve deeper to find another reason for her interest?

'Make a pass at you, did he?' Alistair chuckled, and Mickey bit back her hasty retort. Grant's words to her could hardly be construed as making a pass, by any standards, but still, it did give her a firmer footing for making the enquiry, a more legitimate reason.

'Something like that,' she managed to lie between gritted teeth. 'Anyway his name's Grant . . . Keir Grant,' she added quickly, remembering what the photographer had called him.

There was a moment's silence, then the soft, sibilant sound of Alistair letting out a low whistle.

'So, he's here, is he? He must have slipped in without us noticing his name on the flight roster . . . That was careless.'

There was no mistaking the interest in the man's voice, and a shiver of unease raced down her spine as she heard it. Good heavens, what had she done? If Grant had been trying to keep his visit quiet and found out that she'd been the one to tip off the papers, then there was just no knowing what might happen. But still, it was done now, and there was little she could do to change it beyond finding out as much as she could about him.

'Who is he?' she asked, leaning a shoulder against the wall, her knees suddenly strangely weak.

'He owns a huge salvage operation in the States. Rumour has it he's the American dream . . . the self-made man who dragged himself up from deckhand on some old tub to owner of a multi-million dollar company. He was in charge of bringing that consignment of gold bars up from the North Atlantic coast last year. You must remember it, Mickey, it was in all the papers and had extensive television coverage.'

'Of course.'

Her mind quickly raced back in time. The story had held the public's imagination for nigh on a week, and she'd followed it with as much interest as anyone. No wonder he thought she must know who he was; pictures of him had featured heavily in the media coverage, but he'd been clean-shaven then, and she just hadn't recognised him.

'Now, I wonder what he's doing over here,' Alistair mused softly. 'Must be something he's trying to keep quiet, or you can be certain he wouldn't be flying 'economy' . . . lack of money is not likely to be something he's suffering from, I can tell you. Why, from that one operation alone he earned a small fortune!'

'I'm afraid I've no idea.' Hastily, Mickey sought to dampen his interest down a bit, but it was to no avail.

'Mmm . . . well, thanks for letting me know, Mickey. I'll make a few enquiries, see what I can turn up. There might just be a story in it. Any chance you'll be seeing him again?' he asked hopefully, and she shuddered at the thought.

'No,' she answered shortly, hoping she was right.

'Pity. Still, you never know what turns up, do you? Anyway, I'd better let you go now and I'll see you when you come in to the office. In fact, I'll buy you a drink for the tip. Bye, love.'

'Bye.'

Replacing the receiver, Mickey swallowed down the groan which rushed to her lips. What had she done? Once Alistair got interested in a story he was like the proverbial dog with a bone. If Grant found out she'd started off the enquiries, albeit innocently, there was no knowing what he might do, no knowing just how quickly he might carry out his threat and release the photographs to the Press. She had to get them back, had to find some way of making him change his mind about using them. Perhaps if it had just been her they could hurt, then maybe she'd be willing to take a chance, but it wasn't that simple. There was Aunt Ruth to consider, and, leaning weakly against the wall, Mickey knew there was just no way she could ever risk anything hurting her . . . she owed her too much for that.

She'd been barely eighteen when her parents had died in a motorway accident, and it had been Aunt Ruth who had taken her in and given her all the love and support she'd needed to face the tragedy. Aunt Ruth, her great-aunt really, had been in her sixties then, but somehow the age gap had never mattered. Mickey had found in her the same warmth and caring she'd found in her own mother and, though she'd missed her parents, Aunt Ruth had made it all bearable.

Money had been tight, though, with only a small amount left from the sale of her parents' house, plus Aunt Ruth's meagre pension to live off, and Mickey had been keen to get a job as soon as she could to help out. Aunt Ruth, in her quiet, gentle way, had refused to let her, insisting that she aimed for a proper career, and finally Mickey had decided on catering. With the help of a small government grant she'd put herself through college, working hard to earn a well-deserved honours diploma.

A few lean years of struggling had followed until, blissfully, everything started to fall into place and come together far better then either she or Aunt Ruth could ever have hoped for. She'd started an agency with a friend, Lucy Walker, providing high-class meals in clients' homes, and this had gradually built up into a very successful and profitable business. There was great demand for the service, and as word spread about the excellence of their work they'd found themselves in more and more demand by a wide variety of people, one of whom was the owner of the paper she now wrote for. He'd been so impressed by Mickey's culinary talents that he'd asked her to write a twice-weekly column which, judging by the amount of letters she received each week, was very popular.

In recent months, feelers had been put out, testing to see if she'd be interested in doing something for television, and after her taste of working on the American programme she knew she would. Her career was moving on an upwards curve, and Aunt Ruth, now a frail and fragile seventy, followed it proudly every step of the way. At the small but well-appointed flat on the south coast which Micky had recently been able to buy her, she kept a huge scrapbook of cuttings on her niece's career . . . and there was no way Mickey wanted copies of those photos to be included in it! Any hint of scandal touching Mickey's name would upset the elderly lady greatly, and there was no way she could ever allow that to happen. There had to be some way of getting the pictures back, surely, if she could only find it.

However, her poor, benumbed brain was just not up to the task at the moment, and with a weary sigh she pushed herself away from the wall. She had other problems to cope with right now, namely setting the house back into some sort of order, and she might as well start by clearing up the broken china. Maybe a little hard labour would help, get everything back into it proper perspective, though frankly she doubted it. Whichever way you looked at it, she'd got herself into to a right fine mess!

Picking up the unread newspaper from the table, she

spread it on the floor and gingerly started to drop the sharp pieces of broken china on to it, pausing as her eyes caught sight of her column. She'd been so upset this morning she hadn't even bothered to check it as she usually did. Quickly she skimmed over the half-page of print.

MICHAELA JAMES'S AMERICAN SPECIALS

As every woman knows, the way to a man's heart is through his stomach, so what better way to tempt that special man in your life than with some of these delicious dishes from America's East Coast?

Chuckling nastily, she dropped the small handful of pottery on to the paper. There was one man's heart she'd like to get at all right, but with something . . . long sharp . . . pointed . . . and *deadly*!

CHAPTER THREE

IT WAS so hot. Perspiration beaded on her forehead, trickled down her neck and raising a limp hand, Mickey mopped it away. If she didn't get a breather, cool her blood a few degrees, they'd be serving *her* up instead of the soup! Turning off the burners, she stepped back from the stove, crossing the room to fling the door open and drink in several deep draughts of the sweet late-summer air. Delicious!

She quickly unbuttoned the starched white overall and tossed it carelessy across the back of a nearby chair, feeling the faint breeze whisper coolly over the bare, heated flesh of her neck and arms in a welcome caress. Four weeks of wonderful American air-conditioning had played havoc with her ablity to tolerate the heat.

Leaning back against the rough, cool stone wall of the house, she let her eyes sweep over the twilight-darkened lawns, following the shadowed line of trees down to the silver shimmer of the river. Everywhere was so still, so incredibly peaceful, that gradually she felt the last of her tension ease away, seeping through her pores with the escaping heat.

It had been a while since she'd been out on an assignment, her schedule had been so packed in recent months that she'd been unable to fit one in, but now that the first surge of trembling nerves was abating she was glad that she had. Oh, the newspaper column, the articles and demonstrations which now filled her days, were fine in their way and she enjoyed them, but this was different; this was the true test of her skills as a cook, and she was glad that Lucy had phoned her and asked her to take the assignment. It got her back to her roots, back to where she had started on her culinary career.

42

The sudden sweep of headlights arcing across the darkening lawns roused her, and swiftly Mickey straightened, shooting a guilty look at the large watch strapped to her wrist. The first of Mrs Forrester's guests must be arriving, and she still had the vegetables to steam. If she didn't get a move on she'd fall behind schedule, and that would never do.

Turning to step back inside the kitchen, she paused at the sound of a woman's voice spilling through the quiet night air.

'Darling, you're early. Couldn't you wait to see me, then?'

There was a breathy note to the girl's voice, and Mickey grinned. In the fashion of bygone years, the kitchen was set slightly below ground-level, with three steps leading up to the gravelled path, and from this angle all she could see of the figure was the fluttering folds of a long, rose-pink dress. However, she didn't need to see more; the cooing softness to the girl's tones had been all she needed to imagine her expression.

Gravel crunched, and as Mickey watched two dark-clad legs appeared, pausing a mere pace away from the top of the steps.

'What do you think?'

There was mocking inflection to the deep voice, a teasing note which made the girl chuckle, mercifully covering the sharp sound of Mickey's gasp of dismay. Reeling, she clutched at the door for support, a flashfire of shock burning through her.

Although it had been over a week since she'd heard it last, there was no mistaking that voice, no mistaking the depth, the soft liquid flow of the lightly accented tones. Keir Grant . . . Here!

The soft crunch of a double set of footsteps crossing the gravel dimly cut through her horrified brain, making her realise that it would need little more than a swift downward glance for them to catch sight of her cowering in the doorway. Carefully, gingerly, she edged herself inside, thanking merciful heaven that she had discarded the gleaming white overall, knowing that the plain navy T-shirt and skirt helped her blend more easily into the shadows.

Quickly she slid round the door, pressing it closed with hands that trembled, desperately needing to set some barrier between herself and that man. Her heart was racing, pumping the blood round her veins in a riptiding surge, and she pressed a slim hand to her throat to stem the flood. She had to think clearly, decide what to do; there was just no way she could afford to panic. But it was nearly impossible when all her instincts were telling her to run, to get as far away from this house as she could.

'Miss James?'

The cool, cultured tones cut through her panic, bringing her up shortly. Swiftly she turned towards the door which led into the hall, her eyes shooting in startled enquiry to the smooth, immaculate face of Jane Forrester, her client.

'Yes.' Her voice was a faint croak, squeezed from between parched lips, and she swallowed hard, forcing a professional veneer of politeness to her face. She quickly picked up the white overall and slipped it on like armour against a threatening attack. Taking one last deep breath she forced herself to be calm, knowing that any thoughts of running away were pure wishful fantasy. She was here now and she would have to stay . . . no matter what the outcome!

The older woman decended that last few steps to the kitchen, fastidiously holding the hem of her cream silk dress away from the floor. Crossing the room, she peered at the array of pans atop the stove before shooting a strangely uneasy glance towards Mickey.

Slipping the last button through its hole, Mickey crossed the room and picking up a long-handled spoon, carefully stirred the rich cream of watercress soup, something about the other woman's unease flicking nastily at her fragile composure. Had she been spotted? Had Grant said something to Mrs Forrester, some slight against her that was causing the woman all this disquiet? The first trickle of icy anger ran through her; if he thought he could make trouble for her, he was sadly mistaken. She'd fight tooth and nail to save her hard-earned reputation as a cook!

'How can I help you, Mrs Forrester?' she asked politely, fixing her with such a cold stare that she saw the woman almost flinch away.

'Well, it's rather a delicate matter.' Fastening her eyes on a spot some six inches above Mickey's slender shoulder, Jane Forrester began, her fingers moving nervously to her throat, twisting the rope of pearls so that they grated together, making Mickey wince at the noise.

'Yes?' Setting down the spoon Mickey faced her squarely, anger burning behind her icy face. If she was going to be asked to leave, there was just no way she would make it easy for her.

Taking a deep breath the woman began again, a slight nervous tinge edging her usually confident tones.

'You see, Miss James, my daughter, Caroline, has a special guest tonight, a Mr Grant, and of course she'd like him to see her in the very best of lights. Mr Grant is—well, how shall I put it?—a trifle old-fashioned in his views. He believes that a girl should be able to cook.' She gave a short, girlish giggle, stopping abruptly as she met Mickey's set face and hastily hurrying on, 'Caroline has been having cookery lessons and is making quite nice progress, I believe, but obviously she's not up to the standard of being able to cope with an elaborate dinner. I wonder if you'd mind if we let Mr Grant think that she's cooked the meal tonight? Oh, I know it's a deception, but such a small one and I'm sure he'll laugh about it when she tells him at a later date.'

Dropping her eyes, she sent a pleading look in Mickey's direction, and Mickey hastily turned away, knowing the incredulity must show in her face. Forgive the deception? Never! It was obvious that poor Caroline must know very little about her 'special guest'. Even

Mickey, after such a short and hardly close acquaintance, knew he'd be furious about being deceived. Her lips curved in a small ironical smile as she realised just how wrong she'd been . . . far from being asked to leave, it appeared that she featured strongly in their plans for the night. But she just couldn't agree to such a plan; the girl must be mad to even consider it.

Opening her mouth to persuade her client that the idea might not be quite as good as it first seemed, she paused, a rather nasty thought slithering fast through her mind. Why should she worry? Why should she go out of her way, and probably incur the woman's displeasure, trying to prevent the deception? It would serve that abominable man right if he fell for the trick. He deserved his comeuppance, and this could be the perfect way to ensure he got it.

Turning, she smiled warmly at the waiting woman, desperately trying to keep the malicious gleam from her hazel eyes. What a lovely way to even their score!

It was a going beautifully.

With the kitchen door wide open, Mickey could hear the soft, muted hum of voices issuing from the large dining-room, and she smiled to herself. It was always a very satisfying feeling when a meal went exactly to plan and when clients were as obviously appreciative as the Forresters, but even more so tonight.

With the serving of every beautifully cooked course Mickey rejoiced in the trick which was being played on their guest, and it was all she could do to stop herself singing for joy. It could only been better if she'd been able to see his face when he realised just how he'd been deceived, and just who had played such a major part in the plan. But still, she couldn't have everything, and even this tiny act of revenge would help her sleep easier each night than she'd done since he'd paid that visit to her house. Whoever had said revenge was sweet had most definitely known what he was talking about!

Humming gently to herself, Mickey opened the fridge

door and slid the large tray of champagne glasses from the top shelf, setting it carefully down on the side of the big scrubbed pine table.

Whenever a booking was accepted, the agency made certain that the clients understood not everything could be cooked in their homes in the limited time available. One or two courses were always prepared in advance, as Mickey had done with the soup and this delicious light gooseberry fool for dessert. Now all that was left to complete it was the swirl of rich double cream she would add for decoration

Picking up the large piping bag, she set to work, rimming the wide-mouthed glasses with intricate patterns of cream. The soft clatter of footsteps coming down the stairs made her pause and she looked towards the door, her eyes sweeping over the tall, elegant blonde figure of Caroline Forrester.

'How is it going?' she enquired politely, before turning her attention back to the next dish.

'Oh, marvellous. Keir was really impressed with the beef Wellington,' she chuckled softly. 'He's such a tease, Miss James. Why, he's just said he'll have to give me a better score for cooking such a wonderful meal.'

Turning, she executed several happy spins around the table, mercifully missing the expression on Mickey's face.

The poor, besotted girl thought he was teasing, but *she* knew better. Why, probably the numbers were being added up in that computer mind of his even now; so many for the beef, so many for the vegetables . . . The man was unbelievable! It made her blood boil to think how the girl was being judged, but there was little she could do about it.

Taking a deep breath, she forced herself to be calm, knowing that her inward agitation was having disastrous effects on her piping technique. Quickly and deftly she added the last flourish to the final glass, before lifting the bag clear and setting it down in the bowl.

'That looks lovely, Miss James. I don't know how you manage to pipe the cream on like that. Whenever I've tried it just wells into one sticky mass.'

Stopping her pirouettes, Caroline stood and admired the dishes, and Mickey smiled warmly at her. She was a nice girl, despite her obviously poor taste in men!

'It's just a knack, really. You'll get better at it the more you practise,' she assured her.

'Oh, I doubt it. To tell the truth, I hate cooking, but Mummy insisted I learn when she heard Keir's views, so I'm struggling on. But there's no way I'll ever be able to turn out anything like you prepared tonight, not in a million years. Why, even the pattern on that glass of fool is beyond me!'

With a slim, rose-tipped finger, she pointed towards one of the dishes, and instinctively Mickey dropped her gaze to it, her eyes widening in sudden horror.

'I think I'll give that one to Keir,'

Whisking up the loaded tray, Caroline walked quickly from the room, before Mickey could gather her scattered senses enough to stop her, For a full ten seconds she stood rooted to the spot, before suddenly waking from her trance. She had to stop Caroline from giving that dish to Grant . . . or it could be the end of everyone's plans!

Leaping forwards she raced up the steps and along the passage, pausing with a groan of dismay as she saw the edge of the rose-pink dress whisk through the dining-room door. She was too late, there was no way she could stop her now, but she had to see what happened, had to see if he realised her piping held more than just a few decorative loops and curls.

Slipping off her low-heeled shoes, she tiptoed stealthily along the passage and peered round the door.

Screens had been unfolded across the doorway and she carefully edged inside and peered through a gap in them, jerking back in alarm as she spotted the tall, familiar, bearded figure seated opposite. Her heart was pounding high in her throat and she swallowed hard, silently berating herself for being so stupid. There was no way he could see her, or know she was there, and she quickly settled back to her peep-hole.

Caroline had served all the dishes now, and Mickey held her breath as she watched him pick up the silver spoon, his attention centred on something his hostess was saying. He idly twirled the delicate glass on its fine china saucer, and Mickey felt her nerves knot into tense ropes. Then with a low laugh he dropped his gaze, swooping the spoon towards the dish, and for one glorious moment she thought he'd missed it. Hope rushed through her in a great flood, to be quickly damned as the spoon halted abruptly a mere fraction away from the dish. Mickey felt the ground tilt towards her as she saw the rapid play of emotions which crossed his face. Closing her eyes, she reeled back against the wall for support, a freeze-frame picture of the glass surging into her stricken brain.

'10/10.' In rich pale cream the score stood out in all its glory, surrounded by several swirls and flourishes, but quite unmistakable, all the same. Now he'd seen it, he'd read it . . . the question was, would he know who'd done it? She had to find out!

Dry-mouthed, heart leaping, she inched forwards, almost afraid to see what might happen.

He'd turned his attention to Caroline now, blue eyes sweeping over the smooth curves of her innocently smiling face with a hint of puzzlement in their depths as he tapped the bowl of his spoon against the side of the glass dish, and Mickey had to bite back a small, nervous chuckle of laughter as she understood his confusion.

He'd seen the score, all right, but really couldn't believe that Caroline had done it, and no wonder; even with what little she knew of the girl, Mickey knew that it was most unlikely she'd play such a trick, unlikely that she would pick him up on his earlier comments about giving her a score and tease him with them. She was far too quiet, too well-bred for such jokes. Still, with a bit of luck he'd soon decide that it had all just been a mistake, a slip of the hand, an extra flourish with the cream which looked like something, but was really nothing. All it needed was that tiny bit of luck, and the fact that he had no idea who had cooked the meal, and never would if she kept out of the way.

Reassured that all would be well, Mickey turned to tiptoe from the room, her elbow brushing briefly against the back of the screens, making them wobble so that the narrow gap between the sections opened a few inches wider. The movement immediately drew Grant's attention, and for one startled second Mickey found her eyes locked with his across the width of the room. In that instant she saw the puzzlement ease from his face, to be replaced by a look of complete and total understanding. Reaching forwards, he lifted his wineglass, raising it towards her in a mocking toast before slowly the screens settled back into place, leaving her standing petrified with horror.

Now he knew who had done it, knew whose hand had piped that creamy score, and she had the horrible sinking feeling it would mean just one thing for her . . . Trouble!

CHAPTER FOUR

SPOON, whisk, spatula, knife . . . quickly Mickey packed her bag, shooting an anxious glance across the room to check the time on the big wall-mounted clock. Fifteen minutes! It had already taken her fifteen minutes to clear up her things, and she groaned in dismay. At this rate they'd have finished even the cheese before she got away from the house, and then heaven alone knew what would happen once he was on the move again. There was absolutely no doubt in her mind that he'd understood what had gone on—the expression on his face had been all too revealing—and she held little hope that he'd forgive her for her part in the plan. No, she had the nasty feeling that he would hold her more than partly to blame, given her previous record for meddling. But if she could just get away before he saw her again then he'd have a great deal of difficulty in actually proving her guilt.

Running a last look around the room, she checked she'd left nothing behind except the short note to Mrs Forrester explaining that she'd just had to rush off. If her client thought her rapid departure a touch strange, it was just too bad; there was no way she was going to wait around and let him catch her.

Looping the strap of the tote-bag over her shoulder, she settled the glasses more firmly on to her nose then bent to lift the cardboard box full of dishes up from the table, groaning miserably under its weight. Thank heavens her car was parked just a short way along the back drive, or she'd be the only cook with six-foot-long-arms if she had to carry this lot very far! However, there was no way she could take the chance of splitting the load and making two journeys; that would be pushing her luck just a little too far.

Awkwardly she elbowed the back door open and made her way outside to carefully mount the shallow steps up to the drive, stumbling slightly as the heel of her shoe caught on a small hillock of loose stones in her haste. Casting a furtive look all around before leaving the comparative safety of the house, she crunched her way across to her car, arms straining and trembling with the weight of the load.

Manoeuvring the box with all the skill of a juggler, she managed to slip the key into the lock, but soon found it impossible to press the release catch and open the boot, and she cursed softly. If she put this cargo down on the ground she might never find the strength to lift it up again.

'Allow me.'

The deep, masculine voice cut softly through the still night air, and Mickey yelped in alarm, watching with horror-widened eyes as a large, tanned had slid past her shoulder to press the catch and let the boot gape open with all the appeal of an empty coffin. Slowly, despairingly, she turned her head, her eyes running over the tall figure standing behind her, and he smiled wolfishly back.

'Startled, Miss James? Why, I wonder? After all, my appearance can hardly be a shock to you.'

A cold glint shone in his eyes and Mickey gulped, her gaze running over and past him, as though searching for some way of escape. But there was none. He was watching her with all the keen concentration of a huntsman who'd just set his sights on his prey. There would be no way she'd manage to get past him now.

Stepping forwards, he lifted the box from her arms and stowed it neatly in the back of the car, before turning his gaze back to study the moonlit-pale curve of her cheek. Mickey hastily set several paces between them, willing herself to think calmly and rationally. The only way to handle this, now she'd been caught, was to brazen it out . . . if she just had the nerve. Taking a deep breath, she parted her lips into something which was meant to resemble a smile.

'Thank you. Did you enjoy your meal, Mr Grant?' There was a quavery note to her voice, but she determinedly ignored it, squaring her shoulders and drawing herself up to her full height, which at five foot and three inches was hardly impressive, and negligible compared to his. But no matter, there was no way she'd give him the satisfaction of knowing just how nervous she felt at this encounter.

'Yes, you're an excellent cook, Miss James, really excellent, though just out of interest, did Caroline cook any of the meal herself tonight?'

Although his voice was low, there was an icy tone to it which boded no good for the poor girl, and Mickey desperately tried to think up an excuse for her; but it was frankly hopeless. With his eyes pinning her like a trapped butterfly, she was incapable of finding any reply other than the truth, and wordlessly shook her head.

'No. I thought not.'

'She is having lessons.' Anxious to save the poor girl, Mickey rushed on, 'After all, you must realise that she only did it to impress you . . . she's obviously very attracted to you.'

'Or to my money,' he replied easily, a cynical twist to his carved lips.

'Oh, you can't mean that!'

Horrified, Mickey took a step forwards, forgetting all caution in her anxiety to clear the poor girl's name.

'No?' Raising a thick, quizzical eyebrow, he studied her soft, uptilted face for a second. 'Does that mean you'd find me attractive then, even if I was poor?' he queried mockingly.

'Of course . . . I mean, no . . . I mean money . . . Mr Grant, this has absolutely nothing to do with you and me!' Blushing hotly, Mickey tore her eyes away, feeling the embarrassment well up inside her. He had this annoying ability to disconcert her totally! Hastily she rushed on to cover her confusion.

'Look, Mr Grant, I'm sorry about tonight, but I'm certain that Caroline meant no harm. I'm sure she intended to tell you about it at some later date.'

'Really?' And when do you think that would be . . . after I'd placed the wedding ring on her finger?'

His voice was tightly controlled, each syllable carefully stressed, and suddenly she realised just how angry he was behind that cold façade. But it was incredible; was he really admitting that he'd considered marrying the girl, and then abruptly changed his plans because of one small, ill-considered incident? It was sheer folly, and she quickly tried to make him see sense.

'But you can't really mean that you're going to let this little . . . trick change all your plans? Surely if you love Caroline and want to marry her, this should make absolutely no difference?'

'Who said anything about "love", Miss James?' he queried softly, a mocking light in his eyes.

'But why on earth would you want to marry her if you don't love her?' Totally stunned by his words, Mickey leant against the side of the car.

'Because I felt she matched my requirements.'

For a few seconds she stared dumbly up into his handsome face till suddenly it hit her just what he meant. In a tumbling whirl it all fitted together, the answer to the puzzle which had bothered her for the past week, and she raised a slim hand to stifle the explosive gasp on her lips. Those score sheets she'd read on the plane were his way of selecting a wife!

'Shocked, Miss James?' he asked mockingly as she stared incredulously back at him.

'Yes, if you must know. I've never heard anything like it! Do you really mean to say that you've been scoring girls with marks out of a hundred to find a wife? Why, it's a perfectly dreadful thing to do! What if they found out about it . . . they'd be so upset.' Horror tinged her voice, mixed with a large measure of disbelief at his actions, but he seemed unperturbed when he answered.

'But there's no reason they should find out, is there? After all, there's only two people who know about my plan . . . me and *you*!'

Mickey felt ice slither down her spine at the harsh note in his deep voice and shivered. There was no chance he'd forgive her snooping now, not after she'd finally put two and and two together and come up with such a remarkable score! Her hopes of getting those photographs back must have disappeared totally by now, and there was absolutely nothing more she could do about it. Swallowing hard, she turned away, raising her arms to snap the boot lid closed with a dull final thud before walking slowly around to the driver's door and slipping inside.

'Miss James.'

Bending, he fastened a lean, strong hand around the car door, stopping her from closing it, and she looked warily up at him.

'Yes? Look, Mr Grant, I've had a busy day, I'm tired and I want to go home. What do you want now?'

'Actually, I thought it might be something that you'd want.'

'Pardon?'

Puzzled, Mickey stared up into the face poised so close to her own, breathing in deeply as the faint, delicious tang of some expensive cologne wafted to her nostrils. She quickly ran a glance over the carved planes of his face, and bit back a tiny sigh of regret; what a pity that behind such a devastatingly handsome exterior lurked the mind of a cold and scheming monster.

'The photographs, Miss James . . . and I must say they are quite charming. We make a very loving couple on film.'

'We don't make anything, Mr Grant,' she said tartly, turning to fit the key into the ignition. 'I've already told you that I won't breathe a word of what I know to anyone.'

'Perhaps not consciously,' he conceded, 'but how about unconsciously? That slip—and I take it it *was* a slip tonight—was most revealing. What if you talk in your sleep?'

'Well, there'll be no one there to hear, so don't worry,' she snapped back, and instantly regretted her reply as she saw the laughter sparkle in his eyes. Damn him! He'd been searching out more details of her private life, and she'd fallen for it, hook, line and concrete sinker!

'Well, that's one little query cleared up, anyway. We'd not been able to find out much about your love-like before,' he replied easily, and she curled her fingers tight around the steering wheel to stop herself slapping that mocking face. The man was a menace, a pest, a . . . What had he said? She rounded on him.

'What do you mean, you'd not been able to find much about my love-life? What have you been doing? Have you had me investigated?' her voice rose several octaves to a shrill scream, and she saw him wince. Fury ripped through her, and with a swift movement she pushed herself from the car, forcing him to take several steps backwards.

'Well,' she demanded, 'have you?'

'Of course,' he replied calmly, obviously not at all put-out by her display of temper. 'Haven't you made some enquires about me? I'd be disappointed if you hadn't.

Alistair . . . the name flicked fast through her brain and she gulped, feeling some of the hot temper subside. Obviously he'd have wanted to find out more facts about her as she'd wanted to find out more about him.

'Well?'

'Yes.'

'Good. Then that puts us on an even footing.'

'Not very even while you're holding those photos,' she snapped nastily.

'Yes, I can see how that might be a worry to you. But I have a proposition, Miss James, a way you can get them back.'

A thin wisp of moonlight flickered briefly from

behind a cloud, fully lighting his tanned face, but it gave
her no clue to what he'd meant. She'd bet her last pound
he'd be a whizz at poker. For a moment she tossed the
offer around in her mind, wondering what he was going
to suggest, though, knowing him, she had the feeling the
proposition might be as unpalatable as his previous ones.
But still, there was no harm in hearing him out, was
there? Raising her hazel eyes, she stared up into his face,
forcing herself to act more more calmly than she felt.
She'd need to know all the facts, and view the pitfalls,
before she would agree to anything he could offer.

'I'm listening, Mr Grant.'

Pushing back the cuff of his dark jacket, he flicked a
swift glance at the slim gold watch he wore, before
turning his blue gaze back to her.

'We haven't time to discuss it now. I'll have to get
back before Mrs Forrester sends out a search party.
Come to my flat tomorrow morning and I'll give you all
the details. Here.'

He drew out a thin, leather-bound notebook and tore
off a page to scribble the address, holding it towards her
with a steady hand. For a second Mickey hesitated,
then, reaching forwards, she took the thin scrap of
white, her eyes running quickly over the familiar black
script.

'Tomorrow, then,' he repeated quietly, and she
nodded, turning to watch him walk back towards the
house. For an instant a faint shiver of unease ran down
her spine, till she briskly shrugged it away.

The only way to get herself clear of this mess and that
man was to face both head on. If he had a reasonable
suggestion which meant she could get those photos out
of his possession, then she'd be foolish not to agree . . .
wouldn't she?

The following morning, however, her finger hovering
just inches away from the bell push on Keir Grant's
front door, Mickey wasn't so certain she was doing the
right thing. A proposition, he'd said, a way to get the

the photos back, but how? That was the question. Just what would his scheming brain have come up with, what would she have to do to achieve such a goal? Nothing straightforward and simple, if she knew anything about him!

For several seconds she stood in front of the closed door, undecided whether she should press the button or turn tail and run, till slowly a small inner voice of reason surfaced through her rising panic. She was here now, had taken that first difficult step, so she'd be foolish not to hear what he had to say. After all, she could always say 'no', couldn't she? Squaring her shoulders she pressed the button, before the last dregs of courage could desert her.

The door swung open and Mickey paused, the cool little greeting freezing on her parted lips as she took swift stock of the man standing in the doorway, the towel wrapped round his hips the only barrier between him and nudity! In an involuntary curve her gaze swung from the top of his damp-darkened hair to his bare feet, stopping rather frequently en route to better appreciate the appeal of the glistening tanned torso and limbs, and she gulped. It was enough to start any maiden praying if the answer came packaged like this!

An instense and deathly silence echoed round the hallway, and with a start Mickey broke from her study, blushing hotly as she fast interpreted the smug expression on his face. There was little doubt in her mind that he knew exactly what sort of effect his appearance could have on a poor unsuspecting female, and, if it wasn't for the fact she was so early in calling, she'd have believed he'd planned it just to throw her off balance. However, there was no way she was going to feed his ego any more, and taking a deep breath she quickly brought herself under control, locking her reluctant gaze on to his face.

'I'm sorry, Mr Grant. I can see I've caught you at a bad time. I'll try and slip back later.'

Smiling coolly, she turned to leave, stopping abruptly

as he caught her shoulder and swung her back, a faint teasing smile curving the sensuous fullness of his lips.

'You don't need to go. Come in.' Stepping back, he held the door a trifle wider, but she hesitated, strangely reluctant to step inside his lair.

'Well . . .' she began nervously, running a hand over her hot, faintly flushed cheek to flip back a stray curl of black hair.

'If I don't mind, why should you?' he challenged mockingly, and with a tight little smile Mickey swept through the door. She'd be damned if she'd let him think she was too scared to come in . . . even if it was almost true.

'Through here.'

Quite unselfconsciously he led the way along the small, luxuriously furnished hallway, and Mickey followed, carefully averting her gaze from the taut, rippling muscles of his back and shoulders. Opening a door at the end of the passage, he stood aside for her to enter and she slid cautiously past him, every muscle rigid as she made certain she didn't brush his bare skin. If only she'd left it till later to call, then she'd never have had to face this situation which set her at such a strange disadvantage, but she'd been so full of curiosity at what he might suggest that she'd been quite unable to wait any longer.

'Please sit down. I'll just be a few minutes getting dressed.'

With an easy nod he left the room, and Mickey let out her breath in a sigh of relief that he didn't intend to conduct their meeting in such a state of near-nakedness! Dropping her bag on to the sofa, she sat limply down, her eyes sweeping round the huge, airy room and liking the restful combination of soft, muted blues and greys, the clever mix of antique and modern furniture which saved it all from appearing too stylised. She had the feeling that every item in the room had been chosen for its own appeal, and not just because it fitted into some rigidly structured scheme.

Moving on from a delicately carved rosewood chiffonier, her eyes swept to the bowl of huge white daisies set in the middle of the glass coffee-table and paused with a start of horror on the slim manila folder resting alongside.

'MICHAELA JAMES' . . . the bold-typed name stood out against the pale buff background, and with a sinking feeling she reached a hand forwards, lifting the thin file up to balance it on her lap while she stared down at the typed black letters for several long moments. She knew he'd delved into her background, of course, he'd made absolutely no secret of the fact last night, but somehow it was still a shock to see the actual evidence of his prying, and a flurry of emotion whirled through her till she got herself in hand. With shaking fingers she flicked the file open, skimming over the close-typed pages which baldly stated all the facts about her, and she smiled a trifle grimly. There seemed little to show for twenty-five years of living when it could all be summed up in two foolscap sheets, did there? But still, this was just not the time to dwell on the lack of incident in her life; what she needed to do now was to snatch a look at those photos and see if they were as damning as he'd claimed.

Flicking to the back of the file she pulled out the envelope and slid the pile of photographs on to her knee, staring down at them with a critical eye. They were good, she was forced to admit, good and really dreadfully clear. Carefully she shuffled them into a thin deck and worked her way through, pausing as she came to the last, and a hot tide of colour flooded under her skin as she studied it closely. Had she really entwined her arms round his neck in that fashion, pressed her body so close to his, kissed him back with such obvious passion? Surely not!

'That's particularly good, isn't it, Miss James? I must say I'm rather taken with that one myself.'

The low, mocking voice caught her unwares and she jumped, sending the pile of pictures sliding to the floor.

Quickly she knelt to retrieve them, using the small diversion to cover her embarrassment, and give herself time to get back under control. She must keep icily cool and composed if she was to leave this meeting with what she hoped for. And, having seen that near X-rated snap, it was absolutely vital that she succeeded. No amount of denials would ever convince anyone that she hadn't been a more than willing participant in that torrid embrace!

Gathering the photos up into a pile, she slid them back into the envelope and set it down carefully on to the glass table before turning to run her gaze over the tall figure lounging just a step inside the open doorway. In a white knitted shirt and soft, clinging, grey cotton jeans, he looked totally at ease and Mickey hastily settled her features into a non-committal expression. She had the feeling it wouldn't do to show her hand till he'd dealt out all the rest of the cards.

'Can I get you anything? Tea . . . coffee?' he offered politely, easing his long length away from the jamb, but she shook her head.

'No thank you. I've an appointment at ten, so I can't stay long.' It was a blatant lie, but she didn't care. There was no way she could go through the pretence of observing all the niceties as though she was paying a social visit, when the threat of blackmail was the real reason she'd come.

'Well, in that case, I'd better get to the point, then.'

Crossing the room, he sat down, stretching his long legs out, and Mickey had to force herself not to inch her feet away from the danger of any possible contact. She couldn't allow any awareness of him as a man to intrude on this meeting, or she might find herself in even more trouble. One thing was certain: dealing with Keir Grant made having all one's wits about one an absolute necessity!

'Now, Miss James, you've seen the photographs, so you know what I mean when I say they're very revealing.'

He paused but she just gave a brief nod, afraid that any comment she made might give him an inkling of just how shaken she felt. When she remembered that last picture in all its details, it was all she could do to stop herself hiding from shame!

'Well, I imagine you'd like them back.'

'Of course.' Was it an offer? Hope rushed upwards and she smiled warmly at him. 'Does that mean you've changed your mind, that you'll give them to me?'

A soft flush of pleasure tinged her pale skin, and for an instant he studied her face before replying.

'Possibly.'

There was a guarded note to his deep voice, and Mickey felt some of the hope drain away. She'd been mad to expect it to be that easy; he just wasn't the sort of man who gave anything away without extracting some form of compensation.

'What do you mean, "possibly"?' she asked steadily, flattening out the rising desire to snap. There was no way she was going to sit here and play mouse to his cat, if that was what he planned for the next half-hour. She wanted to know his conditions, here and now.

Leaning back in the soft deep cushions, he regarded her levelly.

'It all depends on you, Miss James.'

'In what way?' Raising a slim, quizzical eyebrow, she forced herself to appear far calmer than she felt, clasping her fretful fingers together in a vice-like grip to hide her agitation and annoyance.

'If you agree to my proposition, then you can have all the photographs back, plus the negatives, of course.'

His voice was low, easy and pleasant, so why did she feel this prickle of anticipation run under her skin, this frisson of awareness of something nasty to come? Taking a deep breath, she faced him squarely, feeling the nervous thud of her heart pound high on her throat.

'And what is the proposition?'

There was an instant's pause, a tiny fraction of time when she felt he hesitated, before his voice ran smoothly on.

'It's quite simple, Miss James. You can have them all back if you agree to spend three weekends with me, here in this flat.'

CHAPTER FIVE

IF SILENCE was golden, this one was pure twenty-four carat. For two long minutes Mickey sat quite still, shock-waves of horror rippling through her system as she replayed his words fast through her brain, checking to see if she'd been mistaken. But no, even a dozen or so re-runs still came out the same; and cold, icy fury ripped through her like a spear.

The incredible arrogance and conceit of the man was nigh on unbelievable! Did he really think that she'd agree to sell herself for that handful of prints? He must think she valued herself at very cheap rate, but he was quite wrong.

'No!' She kept her answer brief and to the point, refusing to give in to the host of vitriolic comments which fought to break free from her now tight-clamped lips. Gathering her bag to her with shaking hands, she stood up, sheer effrontery seeming to add inches to her petite height. For an instant her eyes swept contemptuously over the tall, loose-limbed figure sprawled in the chair, before she turned on her heel and strode stiffly to the door. She'd be damned if she'd stay here to be insulted any more.

Reaching the polished oak door to the hall, she paused, one slim hand reaching out towards the latch as a faintly uneasy feeling trickled through her. Something was wrong . . . there was just something about this which didn't seem right, and in a flash she had it. He'd never allowed her to get away with the last word before, so why had he let her now?

Turning her head, she shot a quick glance over her rigid shoulder, and in an instant the cold fury melted and fanned into flames as she watched the silent chuckles of laughter which shook his large frame.

64

How dared he? How dared he insult her, then mock her this way? For a moment she was at a loss for words, but only for a moment.

'You, Mr Grant, are the most despicable, low-down excuse for a man it has ever been my misfortune to meet,' she snarled. 'First of all you steal my purse, then hustle your way into my house, assaulting and insulting me on the way, and now, on top of your threats to blackmail me, you have the absolute gall to think that I'll sleep with you to get the photographs back. You can take those photos, Mr Grant, and I'm quite sure you know just where you can . . .'

'Tut, tut, Miss James! This conversation is fast deteriorating, and no wonder. Once again you've been a touch too hasty, got the facts wrong.' He eyed her steadily, all traces of his recent laughter now gone, though Mickey had the nasty suspicion it was merely hidden deep inside. She refused to be mollified.

'Which facts have I got wrong?' Hands on hips, she faced him squarely, a hectic flush staining her cheeks. 'Am I wrong in stating that you're trying to blackmail me? I don't think so.' Icy sarcasm dripped from her clipped tones, but he seemed totally impervious to it, no flicker of emotion showing on his rugged face.

'No, you've not wrong about the blackmail, Miss James. I've every intention of carrying out my threats to ensure my privacy, but what you have got wrong is my wanting to sleep with you.'

'Oh.'

There was little else she could think of to say in the face of this statement. Quickly she ran her gaze over his hard, calm face. Perhaps he was lying, perhaps, having seen her fury, he'd decided to lie his way out, deny that he'd every proposed such a dreadful thing. But no, there was nothing, absolutely nothing in his expression which could be taken as even the faintest indication of a lie, and Mickey bit back a tiny gasp of dismay as she faced the possibility she might have been wrong. Why hadn't she stayed calm, given him more time to complete his offer? A hot wave of embarrassment replaced her cooling fury as with slow, dragging footsteps she walked back across the room, lowering herself to the settee with a small, defeated plop. Setting herself primly back against the cushions, the perfect picture of feminine decorum, she fought to dismiss her previous outburst from his mind.

'I think you'd better explain your proposition, Mr Grant, don't you?' Her tone was cool and reasonable, though she found it difficult to force the words out through her tight-clenched jaws.

'Of course. I'm sorry if you misunderstood me. I suppose I could have phrased it better.'

His voice was low, unruffled, confident in its measured tones, and Mickey had the sudden, inexplicable feeling that his choice of words had been no accident. He'd known exactly how she would interpret them, known too just how furiously angry she would be on hearing them. It had all been part of some devious plan to throw her off balance, disconcert her enough so that she'd agree more readily to what he really wanted. After all, compared to her previous horrified belief that he was offering to take her to his bed as payment for the photographs, any further suggestion would seem very tame!

The thought annoyed her, made her voice snap as she answered. 'Yes, you could!'

'Mmm . . . and as I said before, I'm sorry if it upset you.'

He shot her a high-voltage smile, but Mickey didn't even quiver; one course of electrotherapy treatment in the taxi had cured her, making her totally immune to that sort of tactic. Fixing her eyes on a spot two inches above his head, she said coldly, 'Well then, Mr Grant, why have you asked me to come? How do you suggest I 'earn' those photographs back?'

Sarcasm edged her voice, but he ignored it, smiling blandly back at her across the width of the room.

'When I made you that offer to stay at the flat,

it was purely for business reasons, Miss James, not personal. I feel that you can help me with a decision I need to make.'

'A decision . . . what sort of decision?'

'I think I'd better start at the beginning, don't you? Then there'll be no more misunderstandings.' Leaning back, he settled himself comfortably against the soft cushions, his blue eyes tracing over her part-averted face, as though assessing her interest, and swiftly Mickey blanked all expression from her face.

'I planned this trip over to England not only because I have some important company business which needs attending to, but also because I've decided to get married. Several years ago I realised that when I did eventually choose a wife she would probably be English, mainly because I find something about English girls very appealing. Perhaps it's that innate calmness, that lack of aggression which they all share—it's hard to know exactly what it is, but there's definitely something. Well, during my most recent visits I've been building up a list of possible candidates . . . the list you read on the plane.'

Here he paused, as though waiting for comment, but Mickey refused to utter a word, a syllable, a sentence, till all the facts were put before her. With a light shrug he carried on.

'Well, over the past week, one way and another, I've whittled the list down to four . . . no, three candidates,' he amended swiftly, and Mickey had a sudden vivid mental picture of poor Caroline, who had obviously just been struck off.

'What I want, Miss James, is for you to help me make the final decision, help me choose the one who will make me the perfect wife.'

It was no good, there was just no way she could keep her eyes averted in the face of such a startling statement. Turning, she met his gaze, hazel eyes locking briefly with blue as she tried to see what he was really thinking. But it was useless, she couldn't read anything in those glittering, hard orbs. If she wanted to know more she would have to ask, have to let herself be drawn deeper into this mad, ridiculous plan.

'How? How can I help you? Surely choosing a wife is something very personal.'

'Of course . . . to a point. The three women I've selected are all perfectly suitable to my requirements,' he stated baldly, and Mickey had to stop herself rolling her eyes in horror. How could anyone chose a wife from a short-list of suitable candidates?

'What I feel I need now, though, is a second opinion, another person's view on each of them. From what I've seen of you, Miss James, you're honest to the point of being foolhardly. I know that you will give me a straight opinion of each of the women, and because we're not romantically involved in any way, that opinion will be unbiased.'

'But why? Why on earth do you need a second opinion? Surely it's just a question of choosing the woman you love.'

'But that's just it, Miss James, I don't love any one of them. Oh, I find them attractive, pleasant, good company, but love is not something I'm looking for in marriage.'

'It's not?'

'No. Look, I'm a very busy man, I don't have either the time or the inclination to go through all the traumas so called ''love'' seems to cause.'

'But it needn't be like that, surely you must know that,' she protested strongly, unable to believe anyone could be so rigidly coldheated. 'You can't tell me you've got to your—what, mid-thirties?—without ever having fallen in love.'

There was a moment's silence, and Mickey thought he wasn't going to answer, then when he did she almost wished he hadn't as she heard the coldness in his voice.

'Yes, I thought I was in love, once, thought I'd found that one perfect woman I could spend the rest of my life with, but I was wrong.'

'What happened?' she asked gently, somehow strangely afraid he wouldn't tell her.

'What happened was that I had two bad salvage operations in a row, and the company hit almost rock-bottom trying to absorb the costs. Several of my chief investors started talking about pulling their money out in case the whole thing collapsed.'

'But how did that affect your relationship with the girl you were going to marry?' Mickey asked, utterly puzzled.

'She, like the investors, decided I mightn't be such a good proposition, after all, and turned her attention in another direction, to someone whose finances were much more secure.'

'Oh, but that's awful! How could she do such a thing?' Mickey cried, leaning impulsively towards him.

'Very easily, as far as I could see,' he answered wryly.

'But you can't let it colour all your future relationships, surely? You have to see that you were just unlucky, you'd made a bad choice, but there's no reason for it to happen again in the future.' It seemed strangely important to make him believe it, but, looking at his hard expression, Mickey knew she'd failed. He'd been hurt, badly so from the sound of it, and the worst thing was that he was going to let it colour his judgement.

'No? I'm afraid I just don't have your rose-tinted view of life, Miss James. As far as I'm concerned, love is not the basis I want for marriage.

'But if you feel like that, why do you want to get married at all? Why not stay single and avoid all the problems?'

'Because being single has its problems, too. Look, let me lay it on the line for you: I'm thirty-five, have a million-dollar company but feel I'm missing something. If I dropped down dead tomorrow, who would miss me, who would mourn me, who would I leave all I've worked for these past years to? No, I'm tried of coming back to empty apartments run by faceless housekeepers;

I want a proper home, a secure relationship based on mutual respect and compatibility, children . . . all the normal things a man wants. Is it so strange to want these things, Miss James?' he queried softly, holding her gaze.

'No . . . no, I don't suppose it is. It's just, well, just . . .'

'Just what?'

'Well, just such a strange way of going about it, that's all.'

'Is it? I don't think so, I think it's common sense. In fact, I'd go as far as to say that I imagine many people do it, but the difference is that I've put my scores down on paper, not just in my head. Look, forget about the score system, that was just my way of getting a clear picture of all the girls. The question is, will you help me?'

'But why me? Look, Mr Grant, if you're still worried about what I've seen, then forget it. You've had me checked out, thoroughly if that report's anything to go by, and you know only too well I'm a cookery columnist, not an ace reporter. I've no intention of giving your story to the papers as my latest "scoop".'

Sarcasm dripped from her voice, but he ignored it, his eyes studying her face with a strange hardness in their blue depths.

'I heard you all right, Miss James, but I'm not too sure I can believe you.' He held up a peremptory hand as Mickey started to speak. 'No, let me finish. I know you're not a reporter, but you still have all the connections, don't you? I never asked you to poke your nose into my affairs, it was your choice entirely, and you can't blame me if I now intend to take advantage of it. I need help, Miss James, for the next part of my plan, and you are, quite frankly, perfect. The fact that I have this little parcel of photographs only makes you even more so. After all, I'm sure you'll be very disinclined to discuss our arrangement with anyone when you run the risk of your aunt seeing some of those photographs printed in the paper. It would hardly make pleasant breakfast reading for an elderly lady, would it? Especially not the way I'll make sure it's presented.'

His tone was frankly threatening, and Mickey shivered. Till this moment the threat of blackmail had seemed faintly unreal, as though it was something she had imagined rather than a hard and cold fact. But, studying his set expression across the width of the room, she now had absolutely no doubt he meant it. She could promise not to tell anyone about what she'd seen till she was blue in the face, and he'd still never fully believe her. There would always be that faint suspicion, that awareness of how much she knew, and that would be her biggest danger. What if anything about his plans slipped out in the future? Who then would take the blame? Mickey had the sudden overwhelming feeling that it would be her, and that was a risk she couldn't take. Having seen those photographs now in all their startling glory, there was no way she could risk them being published, no way she could risk Aunt Ruth's hurt and confusion if she saw them. No, if there was a chance of getting them back, she had to take it.

'How can I help you?' she asked quietly. 'What can I offer that you haven't already covered with your system?'

'What you can offer, Miss James, is a woman's view, a chance to see each of the three through your eyes. Let's face it, even you have to admit that most women are more than adept at putting up a good front, especially to a man, but with your help I should be able to see behind that front and get a true picture of what each is really like. So will you do it, will you help me find her . . . the perfect woman?'

The question hung in the air for a second, and Mickey had the crazy sensation she could almost see the words hovering, framed in a balloon. The perfect woman . . . he must be mad!

'Three weekends, Miss James, that's all I'm asking, just a mere six days and you can have all those photographs back and I'll be gone from your life for ever.'

It was an offer she couldn't afford to refuse, not after all that had just been said, but, looking at him, Mickey knew with a small sinking feeling that it wasn't only that which made her nod in agreement. For, despite all his threats, all the damage he could cause to her home and career she was still strangely drawn to him. He held an attraction for her, one she couldn't understand but one which was undeniable all the same, and one which, deep down, she knew would have made her agree to his plan even without the added lever of blackmail!

The glass felt so wonderfully cool. Resting her throbbing head against the pane of the window, Mickey allowed her gaze to wander across the darkening shadows patching her tiny back lawn while her thoughts drifted back to the morning's meeting.

Had she done right to agree to his plan, or had she just put herself in even greater danger? At the time it had seemed like the best solution to her problems, but later, when she'd really given herself time to think about what she'd agreed to, a host of possible pitfalls had opened before her.

What if he'd been lying, what if there were to be no other women at the flat each weekend, no wife to be selected? What if it was just another plan to compromise her, something more to blackmail her with? In fact, what if it was some warped plot to get her into his bed, as she'd first believed?

Here Mickey drew herself up short, a wry little smile lifting the drooping curve of her lips. Keir Grant had been blunt almost to the point of being insulting in his assertions that he had no desire to sleep with her; she'd need have no worries about that, for sure. After all, she'd already gleaned some idea of his taste in women from his score sheets, and there was no way she fitted into the category of a five-foot, eight-inch blonde! No, her virtue was definitely not the issue at stake.

Swiftly she ran over the details he'd given her once

more, searching for any point that she'd missed. She was to spend three consecutive weekends at the flat, acting as housekeeper while she gained an overall impression of each one of the women who would be staying as guests. At the end of the third weekend she was to give him her views on each one in exchange for the set to photos and negatives. Easy, simple, straightforward, a solution to all her present fears . . . so why did she feel so unsure that she'd made the right decision by agreeing to his proposal? It just wasn't like her to dither this way. Usually once her mind was made up she stuck to it without hesitation, trusting her instincts. But this time she was filled with forebodings and fears that she'd made the wrong choice, allowed the attraction she felt for him to influence her. The trouble was, she had the uneasy feeling that to keep up with Grant one had to be two steps ahead in the first place, not two steps behind, as she seemed to be. She'd have to rectify that, and soon; the first weekend was planned for just a few days' time. She must be quite mad!

The sudden sharp ring of the phone, sounding unnaturally loud in the night's stillness, cut through her thoughts and she jumped. She hurried to answer it, sending a swift, startled glance at the clock to check the time. Ten-thirty . . . who on earth would ring at this hour, unless it was Lucy with an emergency booking? For a brief second she considered pouring the whole tale out to her friend and asking her advice, before she swiftly squashed the idea. It would mean making too many revelations about herself and Grant, and she just couldn't take the chance. Oh, she could trust Lucy, of that she had no doubt, but still it would be better if no one else knew, and that way there would be less risk of anything leaking out.

'Hello.' Pressing the receiver to her ear, she winced at the echoing series of clicks and clatters which travelled down the line.

'Mickey? Hello, Alistair here.'

Mickey felt her stomach lurch with shock as she

recognised the familiar voice. For a second, surprise numbed her brain, before it quicky raced back into gear. She and Alistair were more acquaintances than friends, and never before had he bothered to ring her at home, especially at such a late hour. He must want something, some information, and she had the nasty suspicion she might know who it could be about. Oh, lord, why had she ever alerted him to Grant's presence in the first place? She must have been crazy. However, now was not the time for self-recriminations, now was the time for dealing with the Sherlock Holmes of the social set, and that required a great deal of care and consideration.

'Alistair, how nice to hear from you.' She kept her voice cool and neutral, adopting the professional tone she used for demonstrations, the one which gave absolutely nothing away.

'Thought I'd just give you a ring, love, to see if you'd heard anything from Keir Grant.'

'You mean he's not back in the States?' Thinking swiftly, she knew her best plan was to avoid direct answers, in case he sensed anything in her tone. She'd just never been good at lying convincingly.

'No, he's still here, though he's not putting himself around much, I can tell you.'

'So you know where he's staying, then?' she asked carefully, every sense alert to the possible danger of uttering a wrong word.

'Oh, yes, that's been no problem. He's kept a flat here for over a year now, and we know he's using it at the moment. The trouble is, no one seems to have seen much of him since he arrived.'

He paused, waiting for any comment she might offer, but she just gave a small, non-committal murmur, not trusting herself to speak. She'd known she'd awakened Alistair's interest, but hadn't fully realised to what extent, but it was no wonder. Keir Grant was eminently newsworthy: handsome, dashing, with that touch of reckless strength and adventure which appealed so strongly to the public. A good meaty story about him would be quite a scoop. And Alistair seemed determined to get it.

'So you've not seen him, then?'

'Er—no.' Mickey could have kicked herself for stumbling over the reply, almost sensing Alistair's rising disbelief.

'Sure?'

'Absolutely. Look, Alistair, it's been lovely talking to you, but I must go. I've a terrible headache, so I'm going to get an early night. If I hear anything you should know about Mr Grant, I'll give you a call.' This time her words carried the ring of truth, and she heard him pause, obviously weighing up her answer.

'OK then, Mickey. Thanks, anyway. I hope your head's better soon. Don't forget now, anything you hear, let me know. I've the feeling there's something going on with this guy, and I'm not often wrong.'

Smiling grimly, Mickey replaced the receiver. Alistair was right, there *was* something going on, something even he'd find hard to believe, but there was no way he was going to hear about it from her. After all, it was her reputation that was at stake, as well as Grant's!

CHAPTER SIX

GENTLY, Mickey eased the car to a halt, cutting the engine before running a swift glance over the dashboard clock. She was early, twenty minutes if the clock was right, and for a brief moment she considered driving round the block again to kill some time, before she tossed the idea aside. What was the point in delaying the meeting any longer? No, the sooner she got on with it, made a start, then the faster it would be over and done with. Taking one last, deep breath, she pushed open the door and stepped out. Weekend number one was about to start.

Moving quickly round to unlock the boot, she lifted out a small overnight case and her large tote-bag, which as usual weighed the best part of a ton, filled almost to the brim with all the culinary tools she might need for this assignment. Assignment? Slamming the boot closed, Mickey gave a small, nervous chuckle of laughter as she considered the word.

For the past few days her nerves had been jangling with terror at the thought of the coming weekend, and the only way she'd been able to cope had been to try and pretend that this would be just another booking. She'd done several weekend houseparties before for the agency, and she'd tried desperately hard to convince herself that this was just one more. However, now she was actually standing here in the car park of this tall, imposing block of expensive flats, she knew she'd been kidding herself. No amount of effort could make her believe Keir Grant was just one of her usual clients, and for a brief moment an urge to flee, to escape, filled her, before she sternly brought herself under control. She had to remember just what was at stake, and if it meant her falling in with his proposals to safeguard her future, then she'd do it, but one thing was absolutely certain: the next time she sat on a plane, she'd wear blinkers to avoid the temptation of anyone else's secrets!

Settling the bags more comfortably into her grasp, she walked slowly towards the large double doors of the imposing building, waiting patiently while a uniformed commissionaire rushed forwards to pull one half open.

'Thanks.' Setting the cumbersome bags down, Mickey smiled up at the tall, grey-haired man who was watching her questioningly.

'I'm here to see Mr Grant.'

'Miss James?' The man's lined face relaxed into a smile at her nod of agreement. 'Mr Grant said you'd be coming. He's had to go out, so asked me to let you in to the flat. Let me take your bags.'

Whisking up the two bags, he led the way towards a wood-panelled lift and Mickey followed, a feeling of relief that she'd not have to face Keir Grant just yet flooding through her. Within the space of a few short minutes she found herself inside the small, elegant hallway and looked round, trying to get her bearings. She was loath to appear nosey by exploring the flat while Grant was out, but surely there'd be no harm in checking out the kitchen, if she could just find which one of the smooth wooden doors led to it.

Walking slowly along the grey-carpeted hall, she turned the knob on the first door on her left, glancing quickly in at the small neat room with its large desk and leather furniture, which bore all the hallmarks of being a study. A stack of papers on top of the desk proclaimed the fact that, although Keir Grant was in England for some strangely personal reasons, he hadn't entirely left his business behind, and Mickey wasn't at all surprised. There was something about the man which told her he'd find it very hard to delegate his work to anyone else. He was the sort of man who had to be in complete charge of any situation, no matter how much time and effort it might cost him.

Closing the door with a soft little click, she walked

steadily on to the next and peered inside, stopping
abruptly at the sight of the huge double bed. It was a
beautiful room, she could see as she pushed the door
wider, huge and airy, the sweeping expanse of floor
covered with the same pale grey carpet as the lounge and
hall. The walls were papered in a a gleaming silk-shot
silvery-grey, starkly contrasted by the bold black, grey
and red stripes of the bed covers and curtains. Ebony-
dark built in fitments lined one of the walls, the rich
wood gleaming softly in the pale filter of sunshine
coming from the huge window. Taking a step further
into the room, Mickey could just see another door
which opened off into what was obviously the
bathroom, and from this angle could just catch a
glimpse of the edge of a sunken marble bath. There was
no doubt about it, the master of this bedroom enjoyed
more than a touch of luxury.

'Like it?'

The low, quietly amused voice caught her by surprise,
and she gasped in alarm, swinging round so quickly that
the heel of her shoe caught in the thick wool pile. For a
second she teetered on the brink of falling, till two
strong hands grasped her firmly by the shoulders to
steady her. Sensation tingled through her skin at the feel
of that warm, firm touch, and for an instant the whole
world seemed to stop. Looking up, Mickey felt her heart
leap in her chest at the expression in his deep, burning-
blue eyes. For a second she felt herself sway towards his
tall, hard frame, till suddenly, with a small, aching jolt,
she realised just what she was doing, just who was
holding her, and just what had happened the last time
she'd allowed his attraction to overwhelm her. With a
quick turn she wrenched herself free, stepping several
paces away from the gaping doorway and him.

'Thank you. I'm afraid you startled me, I didn't hear
you open the door.' There was a slight quaver to her
voice she couldn't quite quell, a trace of the breathless
tension which had held her.

For a moment he stayed strangely still, his eyes

lingering on her softly flushed face. Then with a slight shrug he looked away, nodding quickly towards the front door.

'The door wasn't closed properly. It's faulty, so if you don't give it a good hard slam it doesn't catch. I'm sorry if I startled you.'

'That's quite all right. If you'll just show me where to put my things, then I can check out the kitchen and see exactly what I need for tonight's meal.'

'So businesslike, Miss James, I am impressed.'

Mockery laced his deep voice, but Mickey refused to be drawn. Memories of his touch still lingered, still shivered through her skin, making her strangely vulnerable to his presence. She had to face the fact that no matter how much she might despise him for his blackmailing threats he still held a compelling attraction for her, an attraction she couldn't, mustn't allow to flourish.

Picking up her bag, she stated coldly, 'I'm here to do a job, Mr Grant, that's all.'

'Yes,' he agreed, holding her gaze, 'just a job.'

It was only much, much later that she wondered if, just for an instant, the tiniest hint of regret had lingered in his deep voice.

Twenty minutes later Mickey knew she could find no more excuses to linger in the bedroom. She'd already re-arranged the small display of toiletries on the dressing-table some half-dozen times, lining the jars and bottles up with a painstaking, meticulous precision. Time was passing, and if she didn't make a start soon the dinner would fall way behind schedule. Taking one last deep breath, she straightened her shoulders and left the room, walking quickly along the hall, the thick carpet muffling her footsteps.

The door to the lounge stood open and Mickey paused, her eyes sweeping across the room to stop on the figure sprawled in one of the deep soft chairs. His eyes were closed, the hard set to his face for once relaxed, unguarded, and with an involuntary pang she suddenly realised he looked both tired and lonely. There was something about the slump of his body which made him seem strangely vulnerable and somehow less threatening.

Was that what he really was, then, just a tired and lonely man who was looking for that indefinable something he felt was missing from his life? Was his aggression, his hardness, really the result of some inner fear that life held very little in store for him? Oh, he had material wealth, granted, and from what she could deduce he had worked long and hard to achieve it, but at what cost? Had he suddenly realised that he'd sacrificed too much to get it? Was that the real reason he now wanted to find that secure and guaranteed relationship he'd mentioned?

The thought disturbed her, kept her lingering in the doorway, drawn to his loneliness as though to a magnet.

'Did you want me for something?'

The soft-voiced question made her jump, made the colour flood to her cheeks in a pink tide. She'd been so engrossed in her thoughts and fancies, she hadn't noticed that his eyes were open and now studying her closely. Drawing in a swift, shaky breath, she strove to answer.

'No . . . no, it's all right. I'm—er—I'm sorry for disturbing you.'

'Are you?'

There was a strange tone to his deep voice, a slight inflection she couldn't interpret, but which made her feel suddenly confused and wary, and she turned abruptly away, needing to set some distance between them.

'Miss James . . . Mickey.'

'Yes?' Stopping, one hand resting against the side of the door-frame, she waited, her back towards him.

'Just . . . thank you.'

'Thank you? What for?' she asked, startled, flicking him a swift glance over shoulder.

'For coming, for helping,' he said quietly, and she shrugged, a fleeting, bitter expression crossing her smooth face.

'You're the piper, Mr Grant. You're calling the tune.' And she walked swiftly from the room, wondering why it hurt so much to remember that fact.

'That smells good.'

'Does it?'

Looking up, Mickey pinned a cool smile to her lips while her stomach flipped over nearly as fast as the pancake she was turning. For the past hour since that strange little conversation they'd shared she'd been on edge, every sense alert to his movements round the flat, but somehow she hadn't realised he'd come into the kitchen till he spoke. Turning away, she skilfully slid the pancake on to the stack she'd already cooked, then poured more mixture into the sizzling pan, pleased to see her hands were perfectly steady.

'What are you making?'

Moving further into the room, Keir stood close behind her, watching the way the pancake mixture bubbled with obvious interest, and Mickey had to draw in a deep, deep breath to stop herself from edging away. He was so close now that she could feel the heat from his body flow over her skin with a strangely unnerving intimacy she didn't welcome. Forcing herself to concentrate, she flipped the part-cooked golden wafer over before she answered.

'Pancakes stuffed with chicken and ham. I hope you like them.' Her voice was carefully controlled and level, betraying nothing of her inward agitation at his closeness.

'I'm sure I shall, they smell delicious.'

Moving slightly, Keir rested a hip against the marble counter, watching as she added the pancake to the rest of the pile.

'How long have you been doing this sort of cooking, Mickey?'

The question startled her and she looked round, her face cold as she answered sharply. 'Why are you asking? After all, you're the one with that little file of information on me, so surely you have all the answers.'

He sighed, a tiny whisper of sound which might have held regret if she'd not known better.

'Yes, you're right, I do have a lot of information about you, but it's only the bare facts, nothing more.'

'So what do you want now, more details so you can find another lever to blackmail me with?' she demanded harshly.

'No, it's not that at all. I'm just interested, just wondered how you've managed to build your business up to what it is today,' he said quietly.

'How I managed was by working every hour God sent and then some more; cooking in grill bars during the day and doing dinner parties on evenings and weekends.'

Moving the pan aside to cool, Mickey picked up a cloth and wiped it over the top of the stove, needing to keep her hands busy.

'But surely you had backing: friends, boyfriends . . . lovers; people willing to put capital into the venture?' he said sceptically.

'No, there was no one, and even if there had been, I wouldn't have let them.'

Tossing the cloth into the washbowl with enough violence to scatter soapsuds over the counters, Mickey turned to face him, a hint of colour edging her cheeks.

'Look, Mr Grant, everything I've ever achieved these past years I've worked for . . . earned. I've never had anything given to me for nothing, and never asked anyone for anything either, so let's get that straight.'

'I'm sorry, I didn't mean to insult you.'

Straightening, Keir stepped forwards and took her damp hands in his, holding them gently. 'It's just that I'm used to a different sort of woman, one who takes as a matter of course, not one who's prepared to work for what she gets.'

'Well, I'm not like that,' Mickey said quietly. She knew she should pull away from his warm, firm grasp, but somehow she was loath to do so, loath to break this moment of understanding which flowed between them. Looking up, she smiled gently at him. 'If being like other women means I have to grasp and take without earning . . . then no, I'm not like that at all.'

'No, you're very different, but the strange thing is, Mickey, we have a lot in common, you and I.'

'We have?'

His voice was low, hypnotic, holding her spellbound with its deep beauty. 'Yes. We both know what it's like to struggle, to work for what we want, don't we?'

'Yes,' she whispered.

'Yes. We're alike you and I, very alike, but somehow I've only just come to realise it.'

There was a moment's deep, intense silence, then slowly Keir let her hands go and walked quietly from the kitchen. Mickey shivered, turning to warm her now-cold hands in the hot, sudsy water.

Was he right? Were they alike? Did they have things in common? If anyone had suggested it before tonight she would have denied it hotly, but now—well, now, the answer just wasn't so clear-cut and simple. Somehow, now, the thought of having something in common with Keir Grant didn't seem quite so unappealing . . . did it?

Lifting up the heavy wooden tray, Mickey set it on the table and started to lay it for the early-morning coffee, cursing softly as one of the small silver spoons fell to the floor. She picked it up, feeling the way her head started to spin at the action. She was exhausted, mentally and physically, and her only thoughts now were to get to bed just as soon as she could. A strange nervous tension had kept her going all evening, but now it had all drained away, leaving her feeling utterly lifeless. She hadn't realised just what a strain the whole evening would be, nor just how much it would disturb her to watch Keir

Grant and his guest together.

'Miss James.'

The harsh voice cut across the room and, startled, Mickey looked up, her eyes running over the tall, beautifully dressed figure of Angela Baddley, and on to the soft green chiffon dress she was holding screwed tight in one hand.

'Yes?'

'I want this ironing . . . now!'

The biting tone came again, and it was all Mickey could do to stop her mouth gaping open with surprise. For the whole of the evening the woman's soft sweet tones had filled the flat, but not any longer. Now the sweetness had melted away, revealing a harsh, demanding note which grated at Mickey's tired, overstretched nerves. Still, the change had really nothing to do with her, and pinning a stiff cold smile to her lips she answered politely, 'I'll find an iron for you, Miss Baddley, if you care to wait a minute.'

She started to lift the heavy tray up when the woman spoke again.

'I'm not going to iron it, you stupid girl, *you* are. Here!' With a disdainful gesture she tossed the expensive folds of chiffon across the room, and Mickey watched dumbly as it drifted into a soft heap on the floor. For a moment she studied it in sheer confusion; did this woman really expect her to start ironing for her at half-past eleven at night? It seemed as if she must, but she was in for quite a shock. Drawing herself up, she stood stiffly erect, a faint hint of angry colour tinging the tired pallor of her cheeks.

'I'm sorry, but I'm afraid that if you want it ironed you will have to do it yourself.' Bending, she lifted the delicate garment up and laid it carefully over the back of a nearby chair.

'How dare you?'

Stepping forwards, the blonde stood a mere pace away from Mickey, her pale green eyes spitting venom.

'When I say I want something doing, I mean it, and I

don't expect some bit of a servant to refuse. Now get it done . . . fast!'

She went to walk out of the room, but Mickey stopped her with just one short word, the only word in fact, she could force out through her rage-stiffened lips.

'*No!*'

Anger was racing through her in hot, furious waves, casting all thoughts of politeness aside. Oh, she'd sensed a hint of hostility behind the other woman's veil of courtesy before, but nothing which could have prepared her for this. How dared she speak to her in a such a manner? How dared she try to treat her this way? There was just no way she was going to take it. Picking up the dress she wadded it into a tight ball and tossed it back across the kitchen to land at the feet of the tall but not-so-cool blonde.

'Why, you little . . .'

Reaching forwards, the woman caught her a stinging blow across the cheek. Stunned, Mickey staggered back as a sick wave of pain washed through her. For a moment the room seemed to tilt and spin, darts of colour flashing behind her blurred eyes, and she reached out quickly to grasp the edge of the long marble counter and hold herself still until the dreadful spinning feeling had cleared from her head. Raising a shaky hand, she ran it gently over her hot, stinging cheek, wincing slightly as her fingers caught against a tender spot where the thin arm of her glasses had grazed her skin. Taking a deep, steadying breath, she turned to face her attacker, letting her eyes run over her with an expression of distasteful scorn which brought more than a trace of ugly colour to Angela Baddley's flawlessly made-up cheeks.

'If you have any complaints, Miss Baddley, I suggest you see Mr Grant about them. I'm here to act as his housekeeper, not to fetch and carry for his ill-mannered guests.'

It was difficult to speak but she just managed it, holding on to the very last of her control with an icy, desperate determination. She'd never been so angry, so furious in the whole of her life, but she refused to show it, refused to descend to the level of brawling with the other woman. Head erect, she let go her death-grip on the cold counter and walked steadily out of the room, ignoring the fury contorting the other woman's face.

Back in her bedroom, she closed the door and leant thankfully back against its solid support, re-running the whole ugly scene through her mind. Had she been in the wrong, been unreasonable or rude? She didn't think so, didn't believe she'd done anything to provoke such a vicious and shameful attack. Nothing like it had ever happened before and never would again, that was for sure. There was no way she would stay a minute longer in this flat with that objectionable woman. What she would do now was pack and leave, and if Keir Grant objected, then it was just too bad. Agreeing to do these weekends was one thing, putting up with such disgraceful behaviour was something else entirely!

Pushing away from the door, she crossed the room on legs that had suddenly started to tremble and began to gather up the toiletries which she'd arranged so neatly such a short time before. Dimly, at the very back of her consciousness, she was aware of voices in the passage outside, but she ignored them, cutting herself off from what was happening in the flat with a rigid, steely determination.

A loud knock came at the door but Mickey ignored it, too overcome by pain and anger to trust herself to speak.

'Miss James, I want a word with you.'

Keir's low, angry tones travelled clearly through the thickness of the door, but she carried on with her jerky, hasty packing. Tears were gathering in the corners of her eyes, sliding down the curve of her cheeks, and with an impatient gesture she tossed her glasses aside to brush them away. All she wanted was to be left alone, to get away from this nightmare situation as fast as she could.

Suddenly the door was thrust wide open and Mickey paused, her eyes lifting towards the tall figure who stood in the doorway.

'What the hell is going on? What do you think you're doing, treating my guest like that? How dare you do such a spiteful thing?'

'What do you mean?' Startled, Mickey straightened and faced him squarely, though her heart was surging and pounding in her chest. Even without the help of her glasses, she could see the murderous anger which hardened his face.

'This!'

Flinging out his hand he tossed a familiar heap of soft green chiffon on to the bed next to her, and she dropped instinctively her gaze, gasping with horror at what she saw. Quickly she lifted the dress and held it before her, her eyes tracing the jagged, cruel tears which ruined the beautiful expensive garment. Raising her head, she gazed towards him in stunned enquiry, wondering what on earth had gone on. For a brief second he treated her to a look of such contempt and scorn that she had to steel herself not to look away.

'I'd have expected you to act with a little more decorum than that, Miss James. Just what did you hope to achieve by ruining this? Miss Baddley's in her room in tears, and no wonder. When I asked you here, it wasn't so that you could insult my guests.'

The biting fury in his deep voice would have been totally intimidating at any other time, but not now. Now, righteous indignation and quite justified anger were racing through her and, quickly stepping round the end of the bed, she flung the tattered dress back at him.

'If she said I ripped it, she lied. The only thing I did which could have upset your precious and ill-mannered Miss Baddley was to refuse to iron this robe when she asked . . . no, ordered me to do it.'

'You don't really expect me to believe that she did this herself, do you? Come on, Miss James, what do you take me for, a total fool? No, this was your nasty little

plan to make me ask you to leave and let you off the
hook, but it won't work, do you hear? You'll either
follow through with our agreement or I'll follow
through with my threat!'

What was the use? For a brief, endless moment
Mickey stared up into his hard, implacable face, pain
washing through her in great tumbling waves. He
obviously didn't believe a word she'd said, obviously
thought that she had torn the dress as part of some
twisted plan, so what was the point in trying to convince
him? Biting her lip to stop the tears from falling, she
turned slowly away, stopping abruptly as he caught her
shoulder in a vice-like grip.

'What happened to your face?' His voice was low but
harsh, still edged with a trace of his previous anger.

'Nothing.'

Snatching herself away, she tried to cross the room,
but he swung her back, turning her so that the clear light
from the overhead lamp shone straight down on the
livid bruise staining her creamy-pale cheek. Raising a
long, tanned finger, he traced gently over the mark,
stopping when she winced with pain, and she could
almost feel the angry tension risising again in his big
hard body.

'Who did this to you, Mickey?'

Gently, he lifted her chin and stared down into her
face, but she refused to answer, refused to give him
another chance to call her a liar.

'Was it Angela? Answer me, Mickey, or so help me,
I'll shake you till your teeth rattle!'

His fingers bit into the soft flesh of her upper arms
but she was oblivious to the pain as she stared into the
glittering blue depths of his eyes. Wordlessly, she
nodded, and watched as a spasm of fury and pain
contorted the hard planes of his handsome face.

'My God, I'm sorry, Mickey—so sorry.'

He gently pulled her to rest against the warm, solid
length of his body, and Mickey felt the very last of her
desperate control shatter into a thousand tiny, broken

pieces. In a great flood the tears she'd tried so hard to dam surged to her eyes and swept over, pouring hotly down her cheeks, as huge, silent sobs shook her slender frame. It had all been so awful, especially that dreadful, humiliating scene, on top of all the worry she'd had these last few weeks, and she no longer felt she could fight back the flood of emotion which filled her.

'Oh, honey, don't.'

Gently, he eased her down to sit on the end of the bed, nestling her head into the curve of his neck while he stroked her hair, and Mickey was startled to feel his hand shaking. Glancing up through tear-soaked lashes, she stole a look at his face, shivering as she saw the grim tightness of his mouth. He was angry all right, furious even, but with whom? Was it Angela's action which had upset him, or her own uncontrollable outburst of weeping? She had to know.

'I'm sorry,' she murmured, her voice thick with tears.

'Why are you sorry? You've not the one who caused the scene,' he said softly, bending his head to look deep into her eyes. She smiled faintly, somehow reassured by his gentle tone.

'No, I know that, but what I'm sorry about is this . . . crying all over you.' Drawing back a few inches, she ran a quick glance over the damp stain marring the shoulder of his white silk shirt, and a swift flurry of embarrassment filled her, making her rush hastily on, 'I don't usually cry all over my employer's shoulder.'

Keith laughed, a low rumble which curled through her like a warm caress, and pulled her gently back to rest once more against the damp patch.

'I don't suppose you usually get attacked by the guests either, do you?'

'No.'

'Well, then let's call this an unusual night and not worry.'

Raising his hand once more, he stroked softly over her hair and gradually Mickey let herself relax against the hard muscles of his chest and shoulders. She should really get up, force herself to do something, but she couldn't find the energy. It felt so good to have him hold her and feel some of his strength seep into her weak limbs. Closing her eyes, she let the anger and pain drift from her, swept away by the caressing strokes of his gentle hand, wishing she could stay there for ever.

'Are you going to sleep?'

The low, amused question rumbled softly close to her ear and with a guilty start Mickey shot bolt upright, the swift denial halting on her lips as her mouth brushed against his. For a second both froze, startled by the sudden, unexpected contact, by the quick surge of feeling which passed between them. Then, slowly, slowly, Keir moved the last tiny fraction till his hard, warm lips covered hers in a gentle and strangely tender caress, and Mickey felt the breath she didn't even know she was holding sigh from her as she gently kissed him back.

'Mickey?'

Her name was a caress, a reassurance, a question; raising her head, she stared up at him, knowing the answer shone clear in her eyes. With a low groan he dipped his head, covering her lips, kissing her again, not with gentleness this time, though, but with a deep, hot intensity which burned through her, setting every tiny fibre aflame. For an instant she was stunned by the sheer force, and pure sensuous power of those demanding lips . . . but only for an instant, before a flaring passion she'd never know before roared through her and she kissed him back, feeling the deep tremor which surged through him at her response. With a low groan he parted her lips, deepening the kiss, his hand sliding down her back, moulding her, shaping her, drawing her closer against the hard contours of his body, till she could feel the heavy, uneven thud of his heart beating in her chest, merging with hers, becoming one. Then there was nothing left, nothing but he, she and this kiss, and raising her arms, she slid her hands around his neck, letting herself be drawn deeper and deeper into the swirling vortex of feeling.

'*Keir!* Keir, where are you?'

The voice called from the hall, cutting into her consciousness, and in a flash the world returned. With a tiny gasp Mickey dragged herself away and leapt to her feet, crossing the room to stare sightlessly through the night-darkened window while she fought for control. What had she done? What had she been thinking of, to let him kiss her, indeed to kiss him, in such a fashion? She must be mad, completely and utterly mad! Maybe that blow to the face had done more than just bruise her cheek; it must have affected her reason at well. She had to remember just what was at stake; had to get her traitorous, foolish feelings under control. The last thing she needed was to get involved with Keir Grant on an emotional level. She just couldn't handle it.

'Keir . . . I'm waiting.'

The sweet, dulcet voice echoed round the room, and Mickey slowly turned to face him. She would never have believed that she could be grateful to that woman for anything, but she was. Her interruption had saved her from making a complete and utter fool of herself. Forcing herself to stand rigidly erect, she peered short-sightedly across the room at the tall figure still sitting on the end of the bed, inwardly cursing the fact she couldn't judge the expression on his face without the help of her glasses.

What was he thinking, feeling? It was impossible to tell, impossible to see if he regretted his actions, regretted that brief tumultuous flare of feeling which had awakened between them.

Suddenly he stood up, crossing the room to stand just inches away from her stiff, rigid figure and Mickey had to stifle the instant flare of longing which filled her. His eyes ran slowly over her flushed face, and she had the strangest feeling he was fighting some deep inner battle as she saw the torment which etched his face. There was a moment's deep silence, then he turned and walked quickly from the room, closing the door softly behind him. Mickey felt as though a large hole had been ripped in her soul as she watched him go.

Moving quietly, Mickey walked along to the kitchen, knowing she was about to face the hardest test in her life. She'd lain awake the best part of the night, her mind full of those minutes she'd spent in Keir's arms, completely robbing her of the ability to sleep. Why had he done it? Why had he kissed her with such intensity and passion? Why, too, had she responded with such equal fervour? She didn't understand it, didn't even think she wanted to right at the moment. The only way she could handle this next hour or so until she could leave the flat was by staying as detached as possible, though she had the bitter feeling it would be very difficult while the memories of last night were still so raw and fresh.

If it hadn't been for the fact that she knew it would give Angela Baddley intense satisfaction, she would have left immediately, but there was no way she was going to let that evil-tempered woman think she'd won. No, if holding on to her pride meant that she would have to face Keir again this morning, then she would do so . . . reluctantly!

Head erect, she walked into the kitchen and stopped abruptly, her eyes racing to the tall figure slumped in a chair, a half-drunk mug of coffee clasped in his hand. There was a moment's silence when stillness fell over the room, locking them both into some strange, frozen tableau, then he turned back to stare into the depths of his mug.

'I'm sorry, I didn't know you were in here,' she said haltingly. 'I was going to start breakfast.'

'Don't let me stop you,' he answered briefly, a flatness to his tone.

She headed for the fridge, her hands trembling as she collected what she needed. She'd hoped to have more time before she had to face him, a few minutes longer to armour herself, but it obviously wasn't to be.

'Mickey.'

His voice broke the small silence and Mickey jumped, feeling her heart start to leap and hammer in her chest in a wild rhythm.

'Yes?' she answered, her voice strained, even to her ears.

'About last night . . . we have to talk.'

'I don't think there's anything to talk about,' she said quietly, 'unless it's about Miss Baddley's dress and I told you then that I didn't ruin it.'

'I don't give a damn about the dress, and well you know it,' he snarled, slamming the mug back to the table so that coffee slopped over to form a black pool on its shiny surface. 'It's what happened later between us that needs sorting out.'

Mickey turned, keeping her back to him, knowing there was no way she could meet his eyes.

'You don't need to worry about that. I realise that you were just trying to comfort me.' It was the only explanation she'd come up with during those long, sleepless hours, and some instinct told her she had to hold on to it, especially now. To let herself imagine there had been anything else behind those long, drugging kisses was just courting trouble.

'Was I?' he asked, a mocking inflection to his deep voice.

'Yes.'

'And that's all it was?'

'Of course. Why, what else could it have been?' she said sharply, swinging back to face him. 'You can't tell me it was a sudden overwhelming attraction, surely?'

'Why not?'

'Because frankly I wouldn't believe you, that's why. We both know what sort of woman your taste runs to, and I hardly think I fit the bill.' It was hard to have to admit it, strangely hard, but Mickey knew she had to face up to the reality of the situation.

'Maybe I've changed my mind,' he said softly, but she refused to believe him and shrugged it aside.

'Maybe, but I don't think so. You said yourself that you had everything planned out, every point scored down to the last fraction, so why should I believe you've changed your mind?'

'After last night, anyone would be forced to reconsider,' he said quietly.

'What do you mean?' she asked, her eyes sweeping over his face.

'Well, let's face it, the whole night was supposed to run so smoothly, and yet look what happened. According to my reckonings, Angela was almost perfect, yet within the space of a couple of hours it had all changed.'

'But, Keir, that's what I've been trying to get across to you. There's no way you can rely solely on points to form a relationship, there are too many other factors involved.'

'So I'm beginning to realise,' he said wryly.

'Does that mean that you've changed your mind about the whole idea, then?' she asked softly. 'Are you willing to throw away all your scores and reply on instinct now?'

His answer seemed suddenly terribly important to her and, holding her breath, Mickey waited to hear it. There was a moment's silence, then he spoke, softly, with a hint of sadness to his voice which made her ache because it dashed all the tiny hopes which had flared so briefly into life.

'No, Mickey, there's no way I can do that, no way I can just let myself rely on feelings.'

His eyes met hers and Mickey knew that despite all that had passed between them, despite that huge, undeniable surge of emotion, nothing had really changed. He was still committed to a plan which would probably lead only to heartache.

Dropping her gaze, she said quietly, 'Well, I hope it works out, Keir, for your sake, but somehow I doubt it. You see, you've got to be willing to give something of yourself in a relationship, be prepared to take a chance, but that's something you're not prepared to do. If you're not careful you're going to find it will all backfire on you, and you'll be left a sad and lonely man.'

Her words echoed round the kitchen, lingering on the air like some dreadful omen, and she saw him shiver. Then he stood up and abruptly pushed the chair from the table. When he spoke, his voice was flat, devoid of any expression.

'That's your opinion; I still believe this is the only way to go about things, at least for me. That's where we differ, Mickey. I see emotions as something which only detract from the real issues, whereas you see them as vitally important. Still, don't let it bother you—after all, once our agreement is at an end, then what happens to me won't be any of your concern, will it?'

'No,' she answered, turning away to hide the sudden tears which filled her eyes. 'What you do with your life won't have anything at all to do with me.'

And the thought was strangely bitter.

CHAPTER SEVEN

STEPPING back, Mickey studied the loaded table with a critical eye before reaching forwards to slide a piled-up plate of chocolate bownies just left of centre to balance the positioning of a delicious-looking pecan tart.

'Right then, how's that, Rob?' Smiling, she shot the question over her shoulder at the man who was waiting patiently for her to finish.

'Great, Mickey, looks fine to me. Just let me adjust the lighting, then I can start on the photos.'

Quickly she moved aside, settling herself back at the small table which held her notes, and for a few minutes allowed herself the luxury of self-congratulations which frankly she deserved. It was a great compliment to be asked to produce this insert for one of the coming colour supplements, and Mickey knew it marked an important step up in her career. Cookery columns usually held a very minor place in a paper, and to be asked to devote a whole brochure to her recipes was very encouraging. It would mean a lot of extra work, of course, a lot of planning and preparing of dishes, but it would be worth it.

If she could pull this off it would be a real feather in her proverbial cap. She meant to get to the top of her field, and deep down knew she could do it given just a touch of luck . . . and no interference.

The pleasure faded rapidly from her face as, lifting a hand, she ran a gentle finger over the bruise on her left cheek. At least the livid, ugly purple had faded now to a nasty, sickly yellow which she could disguise fairly well with a layer of heavy make-up, but the sooner this visible reminder of that night went the better then maybe she'd be able to put the whole miserable incident behind her. something she'd been unable to do all week. Perhaps that was the problem, though, perhaps it was silly to try and force the memories from her mind when it would be better to just let them run their course and gradually fade like the bruise. Perhaps she should just sit there and think it all through, let herself remember the scene, that kiss, that bitter, sad conversation later.

'Mickey!'

With a guilty start Mickey looked up as the present returned with a bang and a shout. Swiftly she turned her gaze towards the fair-haired man standing across the room, a camera in his hands, and a tiny sigh escaped from her lips. If she was going to exorcise the ghosts of that fateful night, then she'd be better advised to choose a different time and more appropriate place.

'Sorry, Rob,' she murmured. 'What did you say?'

'I said I'm ready for the next lot if you can get it. I don't know what you've been up to lately, but it's definitely leaving its mark—and I don't just mean that bruise on your cheek, either. What's wrong, love?'

Setting the expensive camera down on the end of the table, he moved to hold her lightly by the hands, a look of concern crossing his pleasant, boyish face as he gazed down at her tired, drawn features.

'You look like hell, Mickey.'

'Well, thanks very much! That's just what a girl needs to hear to cheer her up.'

Huffily, she tried to pull her hands free from his grasp, but Rob was much stronger than his slight build suggested and refused to let her go.

'Hey now, come on, you know I only said it because I care,' he murmured gently, and Mickey felt quick tears sting at her eyes at his concern.

Looking up, she forced a faint smile to her lips as she replied, 'I know, and I didn't mean to snap. I'm just a bit tired at the moment, a bit strung up with all this extra work.'

Her eyes begged him to accept the explanation and not pry, and reluctantly he dropped her hands and turned away.

Picking up a stack of clean plastic boxes, Mickey

hurried over to the long table and started to clear away
the food. Although her back was turned towards him,
she could sense that Rob was watching and inwardly
groaned, wishing she'd taken acting, not cookery
lessons. He knew something was wrong, and she wished
she could tell him, but how could she? If she told him
anything at all, it would be too much, and she'd just
never been good at lying. No, the best thing she could
do would be to finish off this photo session, then try to
keep as far away from Rob as possible until this whole
miserable mess was cleared up. After all, there were
only two more weekends left . . . if she survived them!

Setting her mind to the task, she soon had the table
cleared and a fresh selection of delicious dishes
arranged. Stepping back, she shot a swift grin at Rob
who was standing watching, laughing as she saw the
hungry expression on his face.

'Well then, how does it look?'

'Marvellous. I can hardly wait to get a taste of that
pie, I'm positively drooling.' Smiling, he cocked a
finger towards a rich chocolate cream tart, and Mickey
chuckled.

'And I thought that longing expression was for me. I
am disappointed,' she teased lightly.

'Oh, it is, love, it is, but it's just a question of
priorities . . . food first, you second.' Laughing, he
moved forwards and pulled her to him, and instinctively
Mickey wrapped her arms around his lean waist to
return the caress, wondering fleetingly why his nearness
had such little effect on her pulse-rate. She was fond of
Rob, but on the few occasions he'd kissed her she had
felt only a brief flare of warmth, nothing more and
definitely nothing which could match the hot tide of
longing which had filled her at Keir Grant's touch. Why
should he affect her like that when she barely knew him,
and most certainly didn't like him? It was a problem
she'd struggled to solve right through the week, and still
hadn't. Perhaps it was something to do with how she
was at the moment, her age or something; perhaps she'd

unknowingly reached a time in her life when all the senses and emotions she'd held in check without much effort for so long had suddenly reached the point of boiling over. Perhaps she would react the same when anyone kissed her now . . . even Rob.

With slow deliberation she raised her head, her eyes staring invitingly up into the soft grey ones regarding her so closely, and waited . . . but not for long. In a brief flicker of time she saw the laughter fade from his eyes, to be replaced by some deeper emotion and bending his head, he pressed his lips to hers, gently, hesitantly at first, then with a rising passion as he realised her total compliance.

For several minutes Mickey let him kiss her and kissed him back, while gradually a deep feeling of regret filled her. There was nothing, not a hint, not a whisper of the raging, turbulent feeling she'd known before, and in one aching flash she knew that only one man could make her feel like that . . . the wrong man.

'Oh, excuse me. Am I interrupting something?'

The voice came from the doorway and, wrenching herself free of Rob's hold, Mickey turned towards it, eyes widening in surprise as she caught sight of the small, squat figure of Alistair Graham standing there. There was a strange expression on his face, a hint of something akin to annoyance, but it disappeared so quickly that Mickey thought she must have imagined it. Anyway, she had more to worry about than his expression—namely, just what it was he wanted. For in all the three years she'd worked for the *Recorder* she must have spoken to the man a bare half-dozen times, and three of those had been in the last few weeks. There had to be some reason for her sudden popularity, and she had the uncomfortable feeling she just might know what it was. Why on earth had she chosen Alistair of all people to ring that day? She must have been mad, completely and utterly mad. But still there was no getting away from the fact she'd done it and now, well, now she would just have to face the consequences . . .

Lord help her!

Smoothing the wild tangle of hair from her cheeks, she pinned as calm an expression to her face as she could muster and faced him squarely.

'Alistair, what brings you down here? Not to get a sneak preview of my supplement layout . . . surely that doesn't merit a mention in your column, does it?'

'Hardly, though I must admit I'm always interested in what collegues are up to,' he answer slowly, and Mickey wondered if there was just the tiniest barb to his words. Did he know something, suspect something? It was hard to tell, hard to see behind the bland mask he was wearing. However, one thing was certain; she'd have to be very, very careful, just in case.

Stepping further into the room, Alistair let his gaze wander over the array of dishes, pausing as he met Rob's set expression.

'I'm surprised to find you doing the photographs for something like this, Bryant. I'd have thought this would be way below your league.'

There was a challenging tone to his voice which brought the colour up under Rob's fair skin, and Mickey took a step forwards, not wanting any trouble at the moment. There was a little love lost between the two men, so rumour had it; Rob saw too much of the bad, ugly side of life in his work to appreciate anyone who made a living by digging for it as Alistair did. However, seeing the worry on Mickey's face, he ignored the gibe, turning away to busy himself once more with the lighting, and Mickey let out a soft sigh of relief before saying quickly, 'Rob very kindly offered to do this as a favour. He knows how important the project is to me, and I'm flattered he bothered to spare the time for it. Now, Alistair, I hate to hurry you but we must get on. I don't want the food spoiling under the light.'

'Ah, yes, of course, of course. In point of fact, that's why I've come,' Alistair answered smoothly, turning back to face her.

'Pardon?'

'Food . . . that's why I've come. I promised you a drink for that tip about Keir Grant the other day and I was just about to ring and ask you when I suddenly thought, why not make it lunch? After all, you deserve it.'

'I do?'

'Of course. I've the feeling there's a big story in there somewhere, Mickey, if I can just find it, and I'm really grateful to you for the tip-off. So you must let me buy you lunch to show my appreciation.'

'Oh, no, really, Alistair. I—er—I . . .' Horror was addling her wits, stunning her brain, so that for a second all the thousand excuses she could usually muster faded away.

'I won't take no for an answer. One o'clock at the Owls, Mickey. See you later.'

With a speed which belied his five-foot-six-inch, fourteen-stone frame he was out the door and gone, leaving her standing . . . gasping.

'Keir Grant, eh?' Rob said softly.

The name slid like a slow river of ice down her spine, making her shiver with a cold, ominous dread. What had she done? What in all creation had she done when she'd opened that Pandora's Box of questions and asked Alistair to supply the answers?

The restaurant was lovely: long, low and elegantly gracious, with landscaped grounds sweeping down to a small tree-rimmed lake. Looking at it, Mickey felt the first shivers of real alarm race through her. Alistair Graham was positively renowned for his meanness, reputed to have the longest pockets and shortest arms in the business, and if he was paying for a meal at such an expensive place she very much doubted it was just to express his thanks to her. No, Alistair was after more, much more, but she'd be very careful that he didn't get it!

'What exactly is going on, Mickey, between you and Alistair? Just what did he mean about you tipping him off about Grant? It must have been some tip if he's treating you to lunch here.'

Rob's words only reinforced her own opinion, but she couldn't admit it, couldn't let him suspect just how worried she was. He'd been very quiet on the drive over, and for the last hour since Alistair had left the studio, and Mickey knew she'd be hard pushed to find a suitable reply. But she had to try, had to find something which would satisfy him.

Turning slightly in the car seat, she let her gaze travel rapidly over his face, her eyes meeting his before sliding quickly away as she answered quietly, 'I met Mr Grant on the flight back from the States. I sat next to him but didn't recognise him immediately, so I rang Alistair to see if he knew who he was. Alistair hadn't realised he'd come back into England, so he was pleased with the information . . . . that's all.'

'Oh, come on, love, there's more to it than that, so don't try and kid me. You looked postively worried when Alistair mentioned his name.' With a vicious twist Rob turned off the ignition, so that for a moment a deep silence echoed round them, a silence which made her feel even more tense and nervous. Desperately she sought round for something else to tell him, something which would explain her concern.

'Well, actually there was more to it than just a meeting. Mr Grant and I had rather a disagreement over something I'd seen, and I'm afraid we didn't part on the best of terms, though obviously I've not told Alistair about it in case he starts digging for a story.' Would he believe her? Holding her breath, Mickey waited to see.

'Oh, that's it, is it? Funny though, I thought there was more to it than some minor squabble.'

'Oh, come on, Rob, what could there be? Why, I hardly know the man.'

She could hear the disbelief in his voice, but refused to acknowledge it, refused to try and find any further explanations in case she got herself in so deep she sank.

Rob reached out and grasped her shoulders, staring

down at her soft, anxious face for a few seconds before saying quietly, 'I don't know what else there is, Mickey, but you do, and I want you to promise me one thing.'

'What?' her voice was a bare low whisper of soft sound.

'That you'll be very careful. I've heard about Keir Grant, love, and frankly not much of it has been good. He's not a man to cross, to mess around with. He's dangerous, Mickey—very, very dangerous.'

'I know,' she whispered. 'I know.'

For a second the desire to tell Rob all and enlist his help rose up and almost overwhelmed her, till slowly common sense prevailed. She had got herself into this mess, and she was the only one who could get herself out. After all, there was really no need to panic, no need to give in to this frisson of fear which raced in quivering spasms up her backbone: Keir had promised to let her have the photographs back if she kept her side of the bargain, and so far she had no reason to believe he wouldn't keep his word. Frankly, he had as much to lose as she if their liaison became public knowledge.

Leaning forwards, she pressed a swift kiss to Rob's cheek, letting him hold her close for a moment before pulling gently away.

'Thanks, Rob, for your concern and for the lift here. I'll ring you tomorrow about the next session and check when you can fit it in.'

She knew there were a thousand things he still wanted to ask her, but frankly she just couldn't find any more answers—at least, not safe ones. Stepping quickly from the car, she walked the last few yards towards the restaurant, pausing at the bottom of a shallow flight of steps to wave as Rob drove away.

'Well, well, what a surprise!'

The low, deep voice hit her as sharply as any axe blade; Mickey spun round and stared in stunned horror at the tall figure lounging against one of the stone pillars edging the terrace.

'*You?*'

'Me,' he acknowledged, a strange harshness to his tone.

Pushing away from the pillar, he strode down the steps to join her, and Mickey suddenly realised he was furiously angry . . . but why? What had happened to bring that tightness to his lips, that glint of fire to his eyes as he stared after the departing car? It confused her, made her feel suddenly terribly nervous.

'Wh . . . what are you doing here?'

Her soft-voiced question seemed to break the spell that held him, and he looked down, his gaze lingering on her mouth for a few seconds before he answered.

'Alistair Graham phoned and asked me to meet him for lunch.'

The coldly uttered sentence brought her up short, centring her attention on the situation and away from the reason for his anger. Alistair! Alistair had invited him to lunch as well as her, but not mentioned it. He'd set them up, opened the trap, and she in all her foolishness had walked right in. What on earth should she do?

'I take it from your expression that you're here for the same reason.'

'Yes,' she managed to croak through stiffening lips. If only her poor brain didn't feel so numb, so totally overwhelmed with terror, then maybe she'd be able to find a solution to this dilemma. But right at the moment she felt as though every thought had been set on hold.

'Well, it looks as if your Mr Graham suspects something, something which links us together, doesn't it?'

'Yes.'

'And you've told him nothing?

'No . . . except that I'd met you on the plane coming over.' She knew there was no way she couldn't admit that, but she'd be damned if she'd tell him anything more, give him enough rope so that he could hang her!

'I see. Well, it lookes as if Mr Graham is after a story, doesn't is, so come along, Miss James—let's not disappoint him.'

Stepping forwards, he slid an encouraging hand under her elbow, but Mickey refused to move even one step closer, and digging in her heels, resisted his efforts.

'What do you mean "let's not disappoint him"? Just what are you planning now?'

'Oh, nothing that will affect you . . . trust me,' he answered blandly.

'Trust you. You must be joking.' With a quick little flick she removed her arm from his grasp and, turning, faced him squarely. 'Look, Mr Grant, we're in this together, and I want to know what you intend to tell him.'

'Quite frankly, as little as possible, and definitely nothing about our arrangement.'

Realising they were not going to move until she had some sort of explanation, he leant easily against the stone wall of the terrace and continued.

'Mickey, I know exactly what sort of man Graham is, I've met a dozen like him over the years, so you don't need to worry that I'll tell him anything more than I want him to know.'

'Mmmm . . .'

Doubt and more than a measure of worry tinged her reply and, leaning forwards, he caught her hands in his, pulling her gently so that she was forced to take a step towards him. Staring up, she felt a quick tremor of surprise run through her at the gentle expression softening his usually stern face. When he spoke his voice was low, even faintly tender, reminding her achingly of that other night when he'd held and reassured her.

'Mickey, there's no way I want to hurt you, believe me.'

And in some strange way she knew she did. For a brief moment they stayed close together, linked not only by their hands but by a deep, invisible bond of feeling, then with a gentle movement she pulled away and walked up the steps, and he followed. Reaching fowards, he swung one of the wide double doors open, giving her a brief smile of encouragement before taking

her arm to steer her further inside. Feeling the faint
tremor which passed through her, he bent his head and
whispered softly in her ear, 'Don't worry, it will be all
right. I promise.'

Looking up, Mickey gave him a small smile of
thanks, hating to admit even to herself that it that been
his touch, not fear, which had caused her to tremble.
Those brief moments outside had thrown her, knocked
what little was left of her composure quite out of gear.
Why on earth had he chosen such a time to act so
kindly, to make her so achingly aware of him as a man
and not just as a hated stranger? It had been the same
the other night, memories of which still lingered to
haunt her. Then every vestige of common sense had
deserted her till all she could think of had been his
touch, the feel of his lips . . . this same glorious, foolish
madness which even now was threatening to claim her.
She had to find some way to break his spell, or she'd be
in no fit state to handle this meeting!

'My, my, what a surprise . . . Keir and his little
"housekeeper"!'

The amused tones had much the same effect now as
before, acting as well as any dousing with cold water.
Mickey let her horrified eyes skim over the elegant
woman standing just a pace to her side.

'Angela, how are you?' said Keir easily.

Not by any tiny inflection did he show his displeasure
at this unexpected encounter, but Mickey could feel it
oozing from him in great sticky waves, and edged a
fraction closer, wanting in some way to give him her
support.

'Oh, I'm fine, thank you, Keir, as you can see. And
you, Miss James, how are you feeling today?'

There was a spiteful mockery to Angela Baddley's
tone, and in the way her pale eyes locked on Mickey's
cheek, but she refused to give her any satisfaction by
acknowledging it and answered coolly, 'Very well,
thank you, Miss Baddley.'

Dismay was dripping through her in great big

puddles, but she knew there was no way she must show it. She had to remember that somewhere in this building was Alistair, waiting . . . and most probably watching!

Aware that her first litte sally had been ignored, the woman tried another line of attack. Fixing a false look of concern to her face, she said carefully, 'I would have thought this place was a little out of your league, though, Miss James. I mean, don't you feel rather uncomfortable and overwhelmed by it all?' Raising a slim hand, she gestured gracefully round the sumptuously decorated foyer with its antique furniture and expensive fittings, and Mickey let all caution slide. There was no way she was going to stand here and be insulted, be made to feel like some gate-crashing vagrant. Drawing herself up, she fixed the woman with a piercing stare, totally ignoring Keir's low murmur of warning.

'Actually, I don't feel at all out of place here, Miss Baddley, but I can see how you might. I imagine that people here expect a fair degree of good manners from their clients . . . something you seem to know little about.'

'Why, you . . .' Furious, the blonde took a threatening step forwards, but Mickey held up a peremptory hand in warning.

'No, Miss Baddley, I don't suggest you try that little trick again. You might have got away with it once, but not twice.' Although she did not raise her voice a fraction, the conviction in her tone shouted it all for her, pulling the other woman up short.

'Keir, you're not going to let her speak to me like that, threaten me, are you?' she demanded with an appealing look in his direction, but he just gave a careless shrug of dismissal, while his eyes swept over Mickey's face with something akin to admiration in them.

'Well, after all, Angela, you started it.'

'So you're still going to take her side, are you?'

'I told you that the other day, and quite frankly I see

no reason to change my mind about it. Now, if you'll excuse us, we have someone waiting and we'll be late.'

The cold scorn in his voice whipped an ugly surge of colour into Angela's cheeks, and as he turned to go she stepped forwards and stopped him, her fingers gripping his forearm like curved talons. Out of the corner of her eye Mickey could see several people watching, and desperately prayed there would not be a scene.

'Don't think you're going to get away with this! Do you hear me? There's no way I'm going to be made a fool by you and that tramp of a "housekeeper". You'll regret this, Keir Grant, and so will she.' The vicious ring to the woman's voice sent shivers of alarm racing coldly down Mickey's spine, but she fought to keep her face impassive, standing rigidly still by Keir's side.

'I hear you, Angela, as do probably the best part of the restaurant, but now you hear me. If you raise one finger against Mickey, I'll make it my business to personally destroy you . . . got it?'

There was no doubting that he meant his threat, and Mickey watched as the woman's face blanched, leaving her features like a cold mask of hatred. Then Keir took her arm once more, leading her away towards the bar, ignoring the curious glances of other diners who'd been close enough to hear the exchange. Only from the tightness of his grasp could she imagine just how much anger he was feeling.

Twisting her head round, she stole a quick look over her shoulder, but there was now no sign of the tall blonde, and she let out a quiet sign of relief that the incident appeared to be over. Angela's threats had probably been just hot air, the result of dented pride and thwarted fury, but still, it wasn't pleasant to realise she'd just made such a bitter enemy.

CHAPTER EIGHT

ALISTAIR was seated at a quiet table near the window, and Mickey just had time to feel a quick surge of satisfaction race through her at the displeasure which darkened his face before they were crossing the room towards him. Obviously, as she had suspected, it had been no oversight on his part not mentioning that Keir was joining them, but rather a deliberate plan to gain the advantage of surprise. However, there was nothing in the smiling blandness of his face which even hinted at it when Mickey made the introductions, before standing to one side while the men shook hands with an outward show of civility, though she had the uneasy feeling she was watching two combatants begin the prelude to a fight.

Within minutes all were seated around the table, making polite, desultory conversation, and Mickey felt her insides tighten with a sudden rush of nerves. For the past few minutes, memory of Angela's bitter words had claimed her attention, but now the real reason she was here came back with force. What would Alistair ask? What sort of questions and, worse, what sort of answers would he expect? He was nobody's fool and, despite the fact she had a deep-rooted feeling Keir could handle him, could *she*? She was no good at pretence and lying, so how on earth could she cope with his probing without revealing anything about their strange relationship?

Panic rose like bile in bitter waves, making her hand tremble as she reached for her glass and took a long drink of the cool, pale wine. Looking up she met Keir's gaze across the table, and something in his eyes, some silent message, steadied her. 'Trust me,' he'd said outside in the car park, and strangely enough she knew she could. She'd trust him and pray he got them out of this very delicate situation.

Turning his attention to the older man, Keir fixed him with a steady look, and Mickey realised with a sudden flash of black humour that round one was about to start.

'I must say I was surprised, and more than a little intrigued, to get your phone call this morning, Mr Graham; I hadn't realised that anyone knew I was in England, apart from a few close friends whose discretion I know I can rely on. How did you find out?'

It was the question Mickey had been dreading since they'd first sat down. She needed Keir's help to sort out Alistair, but would he still be willing to give it when he found out it was she who had started off this probing? Holding her breath, she waited for Alistair to answer, praying he'd be discreet.

'Mickey told me, indirectly, that is,' he answered smoothly.

'Indirectly? I'm sorry, but I'm not with you.'

Mickey could feel the sweep of his blue gaze roam over her averted face, but refused to meet it, staring down into her glass as though she found the pale golden swirl of liquid entrancing.

'Evidently you made quite an impression on her on the flight over, Mr Grant, but she hadn't any idea just who you were. She rang me to see if I could supply some background imformation on you.'

'I see. So you didn't recognise me, then, Mickey?'

It was impossible to ignore such a direct question and, looking up, Mickey allowed her eyes to meet his as she answered truthfully, 'No, I had no idea who you were on the plane.'

'But you knew later,' he said quietly, an underlying thread of steel to his voice, as though he found her subsequent curiosity even more damning than any prior knowledge.

'Oh, yes,' she replied defiantly, disliking what he was implying. 'I found out all about you later.' There was no way she was going to apologise for her actions, for her curiosity, when it was his outrageous behaviour which had prompted it.

'All about me . . . mmm, I'm flattered that I should have generated such interest,' he said mockingly, and she looked quickly away, cheeks flaming with annoyance. She knew it was common sense to imply that her interest in him had been the result of some instant attraction, but it still galled her, being so far removed from the truth.

'Actually, I rather think Mickey is exaggerating when she says she found out all about you, Mr Grant. Frankly there was a lot I couldn't tell her because there's a lot I don't know. You seem to be rather a mystery man.'

Alistair's voice immediately drew her attention, making her remember just who was the enemy, at least for the moment.

'I'm no mystery man, Mr Graham, I can assure you—just a very private person who tries to stay that way.' Leaning back in his chair, Keir held Alistair's gaze levelly.

'Well, there's no doubt you've succeeded. Let's be honest, Mr Grant, since Mickey mentioned you I've done a little digging, and I've come up with virtually nothing about your early life before you started K.G. Salvage. Oh, there's plenty since then, of course, but very little of a personal nature, and that's what I'm after.'

'I see. Well, what is it you want to know?'

'Oh, just the usual background details, plus some idea of what your plans are for the future both for the company and personally. You seem to have a succession of beautiful girlfriends, but as far as I know you've never married, have you?'

'No.'

'Any reason for that?'

'Just the usual, I've not met the right person yet, but I'm working on it.'

Working on it! It was all Mickey could do not to snort aloud in derision. If Alistair had any idea of what he

meant by working on it, then he'd be well on the way to
getting the story of the year!

'I see, but you do have plans in that direction?'

'Oh, yes, Mr Graham, in fact you could say I've some
very definite plans when I find the right woman. Now,
to get back to the other points you were interested in,
just what do you want to know? Keir steered the conversation into less turbulent waters with ease and Mickey
found she could breathe again. So far he seemed to be
handling the interview with a consummate skill and
expertise she only hoped he could keep up, if and when
Alistair decided to apply some pressure.

'Well, let's start back at the beginning. Where you
were born, family, etcetera. There seems to be nothing
printed on that.'

'And you think it would be of interest to your
readers?' Open doubt laced Keir's deep voice, but
Alistair rushed to reassure him.

'Yes, I really do.'

'Well, if you're sure, but frankly, Mr Graham,
there's not much about my childhood that I'd call interesting. It was just the same as any kid's who was born
in one of the most run-down parts of San Francisco. My
father scraped a living for us doing odd jobs round the
docks, but he was more often at home laid up after a
drinking bout than out working. My mother did the best
she could, but it wasn't easy. There were two of us, me
and a kid sister, and I suppose after a while it just got
my mother down. She ran off with another guy when I
was thirteen, and I can't say I blame her. After that . . .
well, it was down to me.'

There was no emotion in his voice, just a flatness and
total lack of feeling which tugged at Mickey's sympathy
more than a thousand emotive words could have done,
making her want to know more about the boy who'd
became this man.

'But what did you live off? How did you manage?'
she asked quietly, leaning forwards to rest her elbows on
the edge of the table as she studied his face.

'Any way I could. I dropped out of school, I had to. Dad had drunk himself into a near-permanent stupor, and there had to be someone there to look out for Karen. I did odd jobs, anything to make a bit of money and keep us going until she was old enough to leave school, and then . . . well, then she found a job on the other coast, Dad died and I was free of all ties.'

There was something in his voice when he mentioned his sister which left Mickey wanting to know more. Where was she now? Did he still see her? Did she realise just what he'd gone through to support her? A dozen questions hovered on her lips, but froze as she saw the set expression on his face and she knew she couldn't ask them, not here in front of Alistair. Some things were just too private, and instinct told her this relationship was one of them.

'After that I signed on as a deck-hand. There wasn't much else going for a kid who hadn't even finished grade school, and I worked my way up, saving every penny till I had enough for a down-payment on my own boat.'

'And that's when you got your first chance at salvaging, wasn't it?' Alistair interrupted smoothly. 'I dug out the reports on that, and even from what little I could turn up it sounded a tight operation.'

His voice held more than a measure of respect, which surprised Mickey. Alistair had a very jaundiced view of people and few earned admiration from him; that Keir Grant should be one of the élite disturbed her.

Keir didn't speak for a moment, busying himself with pouring more wine into their glasses, as though giving himself time to find the right answer. When he did his tone was clipped, displaying no hint of the emotion which in some way Mickey could sense deep inside.

'I guess you could say that first operation was the biggest gamble I'd ever taken in my life. It came over the radio, a ship holed on rocks a few miles east of where we were sailing. I don't know what made me alter course to see it—God knows, it was hardly the best weather to prolong our journey with a huge swell running, but I did. There was already a big crew there when we arrived, working off a couple of ships, and we had to stand off a way, but even from that distance I could see they'd got it all wrong. There was no way they were going to shift her, she was too well embedded on the rocks unless they took a chance and positioned themselves in a narrow channel in the rocks and took her from there.

'I stayed there two days, following the operations on the radio, till the decision was taken to blast her off and possibly save the cargo, if not the vessel. Then, well, then I radioed the owners with my proposal. They thought I was mad, refused to listen at first, but I managed to persuade them it was possible.'

'But surely it was incredibly dangerous if the seas were so heavy and you were planning to work in such a tricky position? I mean, if you had failed you'd have probably lost everything: your ship, your crew . . . your life!' Leaning forwards, Mickey stared at him, wondering just what sort of man could have made such a decision.

'I could have, but I didn't. Oh, don't get me wrong, it was the hardest decision I ever made in my life, a real gamble, but I took it.'

'I don't know how you could do it.' Her words were low, murmured more to herself than to the man seated opposite, but still he heard her and smiled grimly before saying quietly,

'No, you probably don't, but then you probably don't know what it's like to be nothing, to have nothing. I did . . . I'd been there and I didn't like it. Here was the surefire way to make certain it didn't happen again—the chance of a fortune.'

'And it paid off.'

Alistair's voice butted in to what had become a virtual private conversation, making her pull back and remember just where they were.She was allowing the vivid pictures he was painting to tangle with her emotions and blur her thinking, instead of keeping the whole situation in sharp focus.

'Yes, it paid off all right; with the money from that operation I started up K.G. Salvage, and though it's taken several years of hard work it's now on its way to being one of the biggest salvage operation in the world.'

There was a ring of satisfaction to his voice which Mickey could well appreciate. He'd built himself up a multi-million dollar company from nothing . . . something it took a rare breed of man to do.

The waiter came to take their order, and Mickey could almost feel Alistair's impatience at the interruption. He might have already gained a lot of information about Keir, but he was far from satisfied. Nothing Keir had told him yet had explained the reason for his visit to England, and it was this which she knew intrigued Alistair's curious mind.

The waiter departed and Alistair leant forwards, smiling blandly at the younger man, nothing in his expression hinting at the avid curiosity she knew he was feeling.

'Well, that's been a real help, Mr Grant, filled in a lot of missing details for me, but what I'm interested in now is just what had brought you over to England this time.'

'Business.' Keir kept his answer brief.

'And may I ask what sort of business?'

'Shipping business, of course. Look, Mr Graham, I have the feeling that you already know something.'

'Well, I wouldn't go as far to say that. Let's just say I've some strong suspicions that there's something big going on,' Alistair replied cautiously, and Mickey felt her stomach somersault as she wondered just where those suspicions lay. Nervously she twisted her fingers together on her lap. The next few minutes could be crucial.

'You're right, there is something going on, but at present it's highly confidential. Listen, Mr Graham, I'm willing to give you some information, but only if I have your assurance that you won't print anything till I give you the word. Have I got it?'

'Yes, of course—that is, If I can have an exclusive on it.'

There was no hesitation to Alistair's agreement. Leaning forwards, he stared intently across the table at the younger man, and Mickey felt her breath catch in her chest as she wondered just what Keir was going to tell him.

'You've heard of Lancaster shipping, I take it?' Keir said quietly.

'Yes . . . who hasn't heard of them?' Alistair asked wryly.

'Me, for one,' Mickey chipped in quickly, not wanting to miss out on any of the story.

'You haven't? Well, to put it bluntly, Lancaster is one of the biggest privately owned lines in the world. Their holdings are immense. Are you telling me you're in the market to do business with them?' Turning his full attention back, Alistair pinned Keir with a sharp look, surprise crossing his face when he nodded. 'How? I thought John Lancaster held almost total control of that operation.'

'He does . . . at present. However, he's looking to the time when he might want to relinquish some of that control, and I'm negotiating for a partial merger.'

'I see, and that will be final . . .?'

'In a couple of weeks, but only if no news leaks out beforehand. After that, well, I'll make certain you get the story first if you want it.'

Alistair smiled, a slow smile of complete contentment, before lifting his glass in a silent toast of acceptance. Breathing out a heartfelt sigh of relief, Mickey joined him.

He'd got his story, and from the look of it a big one, but thankfully not the one she'd dreaded him getting!

An hour later Mickey stood on the edge of the terrace, surveying the sweeping lawns with a well-fed contentment. Alistair was still inside paying the bill, and for the moment she and Keir were alone. Looking up, she smiled warmly at him, relief smoothing away her usual antagonism.

'It went well—you handled Alistair beautifully and kept him off the scent.'

'I hope so.'

There was just the tiniest touch of unease to his deep voice which tugged at her contentment, sending a ripple of disquiet along her spine.

'Don't you think he believed you, then?' she queried.

'Oh, yes, he believed me all right about the merger. After all, it's only the truth. But your Mr Graham's no fool, and frankly I got the feeling he knows there's something more going on.'

'He's not "my Mr Graham", and I think you're wrong. What can he know?'

'That's a good question, and probably one you're better able to answer than me. Just what did you tell him?' he demanded harshly.

'Me? I told him nothing, nothing at all,' she stammered nervously.

'Except that I'd come into England, and that's what started him off snooping?' he said scornfully, disbelief etching his deep tones. 'Come on, Mickey, you must have said more than that!'

'I didn't. Really, Keir, I didn't. I just rang him and asked who you were and, well . . . that was enough.'

'Enough? That was plenty. God, woman, how could you have been so stupid as to do that, contact Graham, of all people?'

'Stupid, me? Now look here, you big, overbearing, blackmailing rat! If you hadn't pushed your way into my house that morning, and assaulted then threatened me, I would never have had cause to ring him in the first place.' Contentment was disappearing at a rapid pace, to be replaced by a fresh sharp irritation. 'If you need someone to blame for all this, try looking in the mirror, then you'll see the culprit.'

'And I suppose that you had nothing at all to do with any of it, that you're totally innocent, like all women.' Sarcasm dripped from his voice, but Mickey was now too incensed to hear it.

'Of course I didn't. You're the one with that little collection of photographs, Keir Grant, the one who's doing all the pushing. Quite frankly, there's no way I'd ever stoop to such tactics.'

There was a nice noble ring to her voice which whipped at him, igniting a slow, bubbling fury. Leaning forwards, he caught her chin in a firm, harsh grasp, forcing her head at up till she met his relentless blue gaze.

'I may have resorted to blackmail, Miss High and Mighty James, but you're the one who did the pushing.'

'Me?' With a quick flick of her head she broke free from his hold, her body now quivering with a real live temper.

'Yes you.' Although the physical hold had been broken, he still held her fast with his eyes as he continued, 'Let's face some facts, shall we? You pushed me into blackmailing you by snooping on that damned plane. If you'd not done that, then none of this would have happened, would it? You brought it all on your own head, lady, didn't you?'

Grimly he stared at her, and Mickey could only flounder for an answer. He was right, of course, so very, very right . . . but there was no way she wanted to admit it. If she had only curbed her curiosity, then none of this would ever have happened.

'Well?' he prompted harshly, and she knew from the light in his eyes that there was no way he'd let her escape without an answer.

'Yes . . . but . . .' she started, but he cut her off quickly.

'But nothing. If you hadn't poked that pretty little nose into my affairs, then we'd both be getting on with our own lives in our own way, wouldn't we?'

'Yes,' she snapped before clamping her teeth tight together. If he was waiting for something more, an apology, then he could wait for ever! Turning her back on him she stared mutely across the near empty car park, her insides churning with fury. He was the most despicable, low-down, infuriating, insufferable . . .

'Oh, come now, Mickey, take it on the chin. there's really no point in sulking.'

The rich, warm voice held mockery now, and no trace of his previous anger; evidently winning their verbal battle had done much to restore his temper, and with a valiant effort she fought hard not to grind her teeth together. Why was it that every single time she thought she'd got even, he came up with something else to knock her back down? There must be some way, some tiny way she could get to him, surely?

For a brief, delicious moment she toyed with a few dozen interesting possibilities, each one more blood-thirsty than the previous!

'Well, what's it to be, then . . . poison or hanging?'

The amused question made her jump, and she looked round at him in horror. Was she really so transparent that he could tell everything she was thinking? She must be; however, there was no way he was going to discon-cert her any more. Pinning a falsely bright smile to her lips, she answered sweetly, 'Both seem a little too tame for you, dear Mr Grant. Personally, I think you deserve something better, more inventive . . . something even you will agree is worth a perfect score!'

Turning, she walked sedately down the steps, followed by the low rumble of his appreciative laughter.

The water was hot, deep and deliciously frothy, and with a little groan of pleasure Mickey eased herself down into its scented depths. Leaning back she wadded a towel behind her head and closed her eyes, feeling the last of the tension and anger seep from her.

What a day! Between one thing and another it was a wonder she was still sane. Still, it was over now, at least for the present; despite what Keir had said in the car park, she was still convinced that Alistair had been satisfied with the story he'd been given. She should probably have accepted his offer of a lift back to town just to check, but frankly she'd had quite enough of

both him and Grant for one day, and she'd lied shamelessly that Rob had arranged to collect her.

It had been an unsettling day but, lying in the warm
water, Mickey knew she didn't regret all of it. She'd
learnt a lot today about Keir and what had turned him
into the man he now was, and through this knowledge
had come a deeper understanding of what it was that
drove him to act as he did. From what he'd said, it was
obvious that he'd taken more than his fair share of
knocks over the years, so it was little wonder that he
treated everything with such caution, especially something as important as marriage. Now, after hearing
about the unsettled childhood he'd led, she could better
understand his reluctance to rely on feelings. It was
obvious that love had never featured strongly in his
home-life, so it was little wonder that he was loath to set
much store by it, especially when one remembered how
the one woman he'd felt he'd love had treated him. No,
now she could understand his views much better—
understand them, but still not agree with them. Deep
down she was still convinced he was wrong to try to plan
everything so rigidly.

The soft, faint tone of the telephone ringing in her
bedroom cut through her thoughts, and with a reluctant
sigh she forced herself to leave the soothing water.
Wrapping a bath sheet sarong-wise round her slender
body, she padded quickly along the landing to her
room, leaving a frothy track of footprints on the carpet
in her wake.

'Hello, Michaela James speaking.'

Unhooking one end of the soft terry cloth, she
mopped quickly at the soggy ends of her hair, shivering
as a few strays drops slithered coldly over her bare
shoulders.

'Mickey, it's Keir.'

The unexpected announcement surprised her, and for
a moment she just stood and gaped at the phone.

'Hello, are you still there?'

The deep, beautiful voice rumbled in soft enquiry

down the line, and she hastily pulled herself together, answering in a slightly breathless tone.

'Yes, sorry, I've just stepped out of the bath and I'm dripping everywhere.'

'Now there's a thought,' he murmured, and she felt a quick surge of heat flood through her at the underlying feeling in his tone. There was a second's pause, a tiny piece of time when a dozen silent thoughts passed between them, and then he spoke and the moment was gone.

'Did you get back all right? Did your friend collect you?'

There was just the slightest emphasis on the word 'friend', which for some reason pricked at her nerve-endings so that she anwered a trifle sharply.

'Rob, his name is Rob, and yes, as you can hear, I'm back home safely.'

'Is he still there?' There was a harsh note to his voice which startled her into an immediate answer.

'No, of course not! I've just told you I'm having a bath. Why?' Perplexed, Mickey stared at the receiver clutched in her still-damp hand, wondering what on earth had got into him to ask such a silly question. Not that it was any business of his if Rob or a dozen other men were here with her; it was her house, after all, wasn't it? The thought woke her up, flicked at the irritation which still lingered from their lunch-time run-in, making her demand sharply, 'Why do you want to know who's here? You're not planning another of your little surprise visits, are you, with a pet photographer in tow?'

'Hardly, not when I already have such a beautiful and revealing collection of prints in my possession . . . it would just be a wasted journey. No, I was just curious, that's all,' he replied easily.

'Well, you know where curiosity got us in the first place, don't you, Mr Grant?' she answered swiftly, and he laughed, appreciating how she'd thrown his earlier words back at him.

'I do, indeed.'

'So?'

'So please accept my apologies for my . . . er . . .
interest, and forget I said anything. As far as I'm concerned you can share your bath with anyone you want
to, and as you have so rightly pointed out, it's definitely
none of my business.'

A dozen choice answers chased round her brain, but
Mickey courageously fought down the desire to give
them, preferring to treat his words with the contempt
they deserved. Share her bath, indeed!

'Look, Keir, I'm standing here freezing to death, so
will you please just tell me why you phoned in the first
place?' she demanded crossly.

'Yes, of course.' All traces of the recent mockery had
gone from his tone, to be replaced by a business like
precision for which Mickey was grateful. She could
handle this Keir Grant, the cool, aloof businessman, so
much better than she could that teasing stranger.

'I've got to go back to the States for a few days,
possibly a week, which means we'll have to cancel this
weekend. Can we make it for the following one, or are
you booked up then?'

'No, that will be fine, there's no problem about
changing it. When do you fly out?' she asked politely,
glad everything was back on a more solid footing.

'This evening, in just over an hour's time. I might be
late getting back, so I'll make sure the porter knows to
let you into the flat, but if you'd like to take down my
number, then you can always get in touch with me if
something crops up. There'll always be someone there
who knows how to contact me. Have you got a pen?'

'Hang on.' Cradling the receiver against one bare
shoulder, Mickey scrabbled along the bedside cabinet
for a stub of pencil, and snatched a tissue from the box
to write on. 'OK, fire away.' Quickly she scribbled the
string of digits down on to a corner of the soft paper,
trying to hold in flat so it didn't tear.

'Got it?'

'Yes, thank you.' As far as she was concerned there was a little likelihood of her ever needing the information, but still she supposed it was better that she had it.

'Good. Well, I'll see you then—and, Mickey . . .'

'What?'

'Try not to miss me too much, eh?'

'Oh, don't worry, there's absolutely no danger of that,' she snapped nastily, and slammed the receiver back down. Picking up the tissue, she screwed it tight into a ball and tossed it to the back of the chest. Miss him, indeed! He just had to be joking . . . didn't he?

CHAPTER NINE

'MICKEY, you're not concentrating!'

Hitting the mat with a windstopping bump, Mickey was forced to admit he was right. A beginner should have seen that move coming, and she was far from that. Pushing herself up to rest weakly on her elbows, she peered up at the man who was standing watching, a disgusted expression contorting his craggy face.

'Sorry, Tommy, it doesn't seem to be my day, does it?' Raising her arm, she let him haul her to her feet, wondering what had gone wrong. It had been like this from the very first moment she'd started the practice judo session; moves which usually flowed smoothly and easily with a practised skill had seemed to cost her a vast amount of effort, and she just couldn't understand it.

'Well, girl, I think we may as well call it a day while you can still move, don't you?' Tommy's gravelly voice still held traces of his native Wales, although it was more than thirty years since he'd lived there. He'd been a sergeant in the army, had taught unarmed combat most of his working life, and when he'd retired ten years ago he had opened a training school in the town.

Mickey had been a teenager then, small, shy and delicate-looking. It had been her mother who had first urged her to enrol for the judo classes, fearful that her daughter, with her slight build and quiet demeanour, might be viewed as the perfect victim for any sort of attack.

Mickey had gone reluctantly at first, hating both the idea of physical contact and of violence. However, gradually she had come to see judo as something more, a state of mind as well as a means of defence, and as she turned this mental corner she'd found to her surprise how good she became at it. She had an ability not only for lateral thinking, but also lateral fighting: able to see an opportunity and take it, no matter from which direction it came, with a flow and spontaneity which, allied to the basic techniques, had soon made her one of Tommy's star pupils. But not tonight. Tonight the only sort of stars she was likely to see were those flashing inside her shaken head!

Smoothing her judo-gi down, Mickey gave the man a quick, self-conscious grin, knowing that her performance deserved more than the rather mild rebuke in his tone.

'I think you're right . . . I just can't seem to get it together tonight. Better if we leave it till next week.'

'Sure. I can see you've got your mind on other things. I don't know, Mickey . . . it must be love.'

With a friendly thump on her shoulder which sent her reeling, he walked from the room to get changed, missing the dawning horror on her face as she watched him go.

Love!

The word raced round and round her brain in circles, pounded in her ears, flashed in great scarlet letters before her stunned vision. Love . . . was that why she felt so restless, unable to concentrate and settle to any one task? Was it love which caused her to wake in the night and lie sleeplessly, aching, until daylight appeared? Was it love which made her heart race, her blood scream with anticipation every time the phone started ringing? Was it love which made her miss that damned American so?

No, she wouldn't have it, wouldn't allow it to happen, wouldn't even admit it was possible. Striding quickly from the room, she headed straight for the shower. Stripping off her crumpled clothes, she stepped into the stall, turning the jets to a battering full power before grabbing up the soap and scrubbing hard at her body. Even if it took the rest of the night, she was going to wash that idea out of her head for ever!

God, he was tired! Leaning back against the hard leather seat of the taxi, Keir let his eyes drift closed as the strain of the past week caught up with him. It had been a tough

operation, probably one of the biggest jobs the company
had ever handled, and financially the most successful.
Even allowing for the massive costs of running three crews
round the clock, the profits would be considerable, and he
felt a quiet glow of satisfaction run through him at the
thought of a job well done, a satisfaction which did much
to compensate for the bone-weary tiredness which filled
him.

The taxi swung through the gates to the flat, and with a
sigh he forced his eyes open, fumbling in his pocket for his
wallet to pay the driver. Climbing stiffly from the cab, he
drew in several lungfuls of the soft, damp September air,
glad that he was back at last. What he needed now was a
little peace and quiet, a few precious hours to relax in. He
walked swiftly inside and up to the flat and let himself in,
wincing at the suddden blast of music which asaulted his
ears. Quickly he strode along to the kitchen and stopped
abruptly in the doorway.

Poised bare-footed on one of the counter tops, Mickey
was attempting to reach a dish from the top shelf of the
cupboards and having little success. Her arm was just an
inch too short, and stopping her singing for an instant, she
muttered a most unladylike curse. What she really needed
was something else to stand on to give her that extra touch
of height, and she looked round for something handy, her
eyes stopping in stunned surprise on the tall figure who
was quietly watching. For one awful moment she forgot
just where she was and what she was doing and stepped
back, gasping with alarm when her foot found nothing
solid.

- 'Mickey!' With a roar Keir leapt across the room and,
with a save which would have made a cricketer jealous,
caught her before she could hit the floor.

'Ohhh!' Between his sudden appearance and the shock
of the fall, there was little else she could think of to say.
For the moment she was content to let herself just rest
against his big hard body, while her heart stumbled back
into its ususal rhythm. Under her cheek she could feel the
swift rise and fall of his chest, hear the ragged gasp of his

breathing, sounding strangely as though he'd been as frightened by the fall as she, though why, she couldn't imagine.

'That was a damn fool thing to do. You could have hurt yourself badly!'

The controlled snap in his voice made her stir, and she stiffened, trying to pull herself out of his hold, but he wouldn't let her. She looked up, annoyed, an acid gleam in her eyes which was clearly visible despite the tinted barrier of her glasses.

'Look, if you hadn't come pussy-footing in he . . .' Abruptly the words dried up as she read the real concern etched on his features.

'You really scared me then, honey.'

'Did I?' Her voice was low, gentle, instantly responding to the softness of his. 'I'm sorry.'

'Are you? I think you'd better show me.'

Slowly, carefully, his eyes slid over her pale, delicate features, a light in them which made her catch her breath in wonder. Then, gently, he lowered his head, pressing his lips to her hair, her cheeks, her chin in a feathering of slow, warm kisses, and for a few seconds she was powerless to resist the sheer seduction of his touch. The feel of his big, hard body, the scent of him, the brush of his beard against her soft skin, were working havoc with her control, making her impatient for the touch of his lips against hers, making her ache for the real magic he could spin with a kiss.

Turning her head slightly, she went to capture his lips, to force him to put an end to this teasing, tormenting rain-shower of kisses, when out of the corner of her eyes she caught sight of the note still taped to the fridge; the note she'd written after Angela's visit. The single word sliced through her spellbound brain and body, making her remember the real reason she was here, and with a quick shrug she broke free of his light hold.

Moving quickly, she set the width of the room between them, keeping her back to him so she couldn't see the expression on his face and possibly weaken. Her control was held on a gossamer-thin thread which could snap at any second with even the tiniest amount of pressure, sending her back into his arms to accept anything he might offer.

There was a moment's deep silence which seemed to stretch and stretch for ever, then she heard the sound of his footsteps crossing the room to the door, where he paused, and she caught her breath as she waited for all the harsh words he would utter.

'I'm sorry, Mickey. I didn't mean to upset you. I . . . I . . . Dammit, woman, I missed you!'

The words were wrenched from him, completely stunning her with their force and power. He'd missed her! This hard, cold, self-contained man had actually said he'd missed her! Her blood soared, roared through her body, and she spun round, a smile of joy lighting her face.

'Keir . . .'

The room was empty—he'd gone, and with a dreadful sense of loss she realised she'd just missed something very precious; the first and maybe only chance she'd ever have to reach out and strip away the layers and touch the real man inside the armour. With a low, half-choked sob of regret she turned, snatching the note from the fridge door to crumple it tight in her fingers as she fought back the first of her bitter, aching tears. She had no need to read what it said, memory of it raced through her body, pounded wildly through her head as loud and as vibrant as the red-inked letters. 'Zero' she'd written for Angela's score, but now it should be hers as well.

One long, tormented hour later Mickey knew there was no way she could pass the rest of the weekend without some sort of explanation of that brief, startling statement he'd made in the kitchen. There was no way she could go through the motions of being the perfect expert hostess when those disturbing words were still eching round and round in her head. Snatching up what little was left of her courage, she hurried from the room and along to the study, pausing briefly before she knocked on the door.

'Yes?'

Taking a deep breath to help her composure, which seemed to be dripping away at a rapid pace, she stepped quickly inside, eyes skimming over the neat pile of papers arrayed on the desk, and a tiny ripple of dismay curled through her. While she'd been worrying and panicking in the kitchen, he'd been sitting here quietly working. It didn't seem like the action of a man who'd just made the biggest revelation of a lifetime . . . maybe she'd been wrong, read into his words far more than was intended, maybe . . .

'Yes, what is it? I'm very busy.'

The cold uninterest in his tone was just what she needed to steady her and strengthen her resolve to get to the bottom of this puzzle and, levelling the hint of unease from her voice, she asked calmly, 'Keir, about before in the kitchen, did you mean what you said?'

'What I said?'

Not by an inch was he going to make it easy or help her, but Mickey refused to be thrown and continued, 'When you said you missed me . . . did you?'

There it was, out now into the open, a direct question which just had to be anwered, and she held her breath as she waited to hear what he'd say. Nothing in the cool, set mask of his face betrayed his feelings, gave her even the tiniest hint of the explanation he would make, an explanation which could shift the whole balance of their relationship.

There was the briefest silence, then he spoke, his voice calm and level but traced with just a hint of mockery she wasn't slow to hear. 'Of course I missed you; after all, you've got to remember where I've been this past week.'

'Where you've been . . . what do you mean?' Ice was gradually stealing through her limbs, making her whole body quiver and tremble.

'Oh, come on, you're not that naïve, Mickey, surely. Look, I've been cooped up on board ship for the past few days with an all-male crew. I'm a normal, healthy male with all the normal, healthy appetites, so naturally I've missed having female . . . company.'

'And I just happened to be handy, the nearest available body to hold! Is that it?'

The ice was melting now under the flames of a burning anger, most of it directed at herself. My lord, she was stupid, so utterly stupid! While she'd been standing in the kitchen conjuring up heart-rending images of him pining away, missing her, the truth of the matter was that any woman would have received the same reaction if he'd held her.

'What do you think?' Standing, Keir crossed the room and poured himself a double measure of whisky, sipping at the amber liquid as he watched her across the width of the room, and Mickey felt a sick wave of disgust churn at her stomach.

'What do I think? I'll tell you what I think . . . I think it stinks! Next time you need a woman's "company", go and find one of your girlfriends to play with and leave me alone . . . do you hear?'

The roar of her voice made the glasses rattle, but quite frankly Mickey just couldn't give a damn. Whirling round without waiting for an answer, she strode out of the room, closing the door behind her with such an ear-jolting slam that she quite missed the sound of his whiskey glass smashing as he flung it hard at the wall.

Within seconds she was back in the kitchen, her breath coming in such hot, angry spurts that she wouldn't have been at all surprised to see sparks fly from her mouth. Of all the stupid, imbecilic nincompoops, she had to be the stupidest. Heaven only knew just what she'd been imagining he'd meant, but it definitely hadn't been what he'd just told her! But it served her right—so very, very right. Over the past week or so she'd somehow lost track of the terms of their special 'relationship', had begun reading things into it which obviously weren't there. She'd allowed that spark of physical attraction which they ignited so easily in each other to flare up into something greater and far more important than it really was. No, instead of being angry with him she should be grateful; he'd firmly replaced their relationship back into its proper distasteful boundaries, and from now on that would be where she'd be only too pleased to let it remain. From now on all her dealings with that American blackmailer would be carried out in as cool and impersonal a manner as possible, and she'd start right away.

Calmly, quietly, and oozing with dignity, Mickey walked back along and knocked on the study door, before stepping inside. Keir was standing close to the window, his back turned towards her, and she cleared her throat delicately in case he hadn't heard her come in.

'Yes, what is it, Mickey?'

There was a dull note to his voice which startled her—not a coldness, just a total lack of feeling and, worried, she took a step towards him before quickly bringing herself up short. No emotion, no feelings . . . that was what she'd decided, and that was what she'd stick to.

'I've just come to check out the details of your guest. I'm afraid you haven't told me anything about her yet.'

The professional note to her voice was just perfect, doing more to let him know how she'd decided to play this next scene than a whole full-blooded expanation could have done, and she felt a momentary flare of pleasure as she saw the surprise which crossed his face. Obviously he'd thought she'd returned to say more about the previous little episode in the kitchen, but he was wrong. As far as she was now concerned that kiss had never even happened. Calmly she watched as he crossed the room and seated himself behind the desk, and was hard pushed to hide her amusement at such an obvious ploy. If he thought he could disconcert her by leaving her standing, he could think again, because it just wouldn't work.

Looking round, she spied a chair tucked behind the door, and went to fetch it, refusing to remain standing in front of his desk like some naughty schoolgirl about to be told off. Her shoes crunched on something hidden in the carpet; bending down, she carefully picked up several lethal-looking splinters of broken glass and dropped them into the waste-basket.

'I dropped my glass before,' he stated quietly, and with

a magnificent effort Mickey forced herself to do no more than raise one quizzical eyebrow as she noted the whisky stains marring the pale satin-striped wallpaper. How anyone could 'drop' a glass against a wall was beyond her. Still, it was his business entirely and she sat down without passing any comment, though a whole host of real beauties were fighting to get out. It was going to be really difficult to maintain this composure around him for the whole of the weekend if he was going to come up with any more such lies.

Obviously realising just where her thoughts were drifting, Keir handed her a thin sheet of paper covered in his flowing script, before saying firmly. 'I think this should give you everything you need to know.' And Mickey hastily stifled down a chuckle of laughter. Everything she needed to know boiled down to the few basic facts that the weekend's guest was a certain Jennifer Lancaster, a blue-eyed blonde in her mid-twenties who had obviously run the formidable Angela a close second on scores. But did he really believe that this bunch of sixes and sevens was enough to give her a true picture of the woman? He must do, but heaven alone knew, that if they didn't want a repeat of that other fiasco, she'd have to know more before she could decide how to handle the weekend.

'Well?'

Looking up, Mickey fought to keep her gaze level and allow no hint of the scorn she was feeling to show. However, the faint tinge of red which etched his high cheekbones hinted that she possibly hadn't been quite as successful as she'd hoped.

'I take it, then, that you don't feel there's enough to go on there? What else do you need to know about her?' he demanded harshly.

'Frankly, quite a lot. What sort of person is she, what are her hobbies, her interests? Honestly, if you expect me to help, you've got to see I need more than a handful of scores to go on.'

For a moment she thought he wasn't going to answer, but then he seemed to changed his mind and, leaning back in his seat, said quietly, 'As far as I can tell she's a very warm sort of person, has a lot of friends and is involved in a lot of community projects. She's on several committees: children's homes, hospitals . . . that sort of thing.'

'She doesn't have a job, then?'

'Hardly; she's John Lancaster's daughter, the shipping magnate. She definitely doesn't need to work.'

'John Lancaster?' The name tripped something in Mickey's memory, and she stopped the mental notes she was making to give the thought chance to grow. 'I know, didn't you mention him the other day at lunch? Isn't he the one you're negotiating with for the merger?'

'Yes.'

'So any alliance with his daughter would be . . .'

'Purely a bonus, Mickey. Nothing more. I've never allowed my personal feelings to influence my work, or vice versa, so I've no intention of doing so now. If I choose Jennifer it will be because I consider her to be perfect for the role of my wife, and for no other reason.'

'Of course.'

She didn't need to hear the conviction in his tone to believe that little statement; emotion so obviously played a secondary role in this man's life that it would be foolish to even consider he would let it influence any of his decisions.

'Now, as for hobbies, I think you'll have something in common there. Jennifer's very fond of cooking and, from what's been said, quite good at it too.'

'Oh, well, that's good, but don't you think that makes my reason for being here rather groundless? Surely if she's so keen on cooking, she'll want to cook for the both of you herself?'

'No, not the way I've explained it to her. It's Jennifer's birthday very shortly, and I've told her to expect a surprise present when she comes this weekend . . . you.'

'Me?' Mickey squeaked out, startled.

'Yes, you. I thought you could give Jennifer a few tips and hints; make the two days into her own special, personal cookery course, while at the same time you can get a really good picture of what she's like as a person.'

'And you think she'll believe it, that that's why I'm here?' Doubt laced her tone at this suggestion; surely a woman with all Jennifer Lancaster's wealth would expect more for a surprise present then a few lessons in cookery?

'Of course she'll believe it, and she'll be delighted. You have to remember, Mickey, that she has no reason to doubt it, she doesn't view me in such a jaundiced way that you do. Jennifer will believe anything I tell her without question.'

'Mmm . . .' she muttered, then snapped her lips together before she gave in to a deep desire to say more in the face of such comments. The poor girl must be simple if she believed in this double-dealing rat!

'So you'll go along with it, give her a few lessons, will you?'

Why not? If he believed it would work, who was she to dispute it? Standing, she smoothed the skirt of her green linen dress down over the slender curves of her hips and thighs, before nodding briefly in his direction.

'Yes, I'll go along with it if you think it will work. After all, it couldn't be much worse than the last one I did, could it? And when all's said and done, it will be one step closer to ending our arrangement, won't it?

She walked slowly from the room, wondering why all of a sudden the thought didn't make her feel as elated as it should have!

CHAPTER TEN

'MICHAELA JAMES! The Michaela James who writes for the *Recorder*! Oh, Keir, why on earth didn't you tell me before who was going to be here?'

'Because it would have spoiled the surprise, of course, Jennifer, if I'd told you about it. I take it you're pleased, then?'

'Pleased? I'm thrilled! Her recipes are marvellous, in fact I buy the paper specially to get them. Oh, I can't imagine how you've managed to fix this for me, Keir. When did you meet her?'

'A few weeks back,' he answered quietly, a strange expression in his blue eyes.

'Well, I'm really glad you did. This is one of the best presents you could have arranged.'

Reaching up, Jennifer gave him a brief hug before moving ahead into the hallway.

Mickey was just putting the finishing touches to the table when they came in and after carefully winding the last fold of the cream damask napkin into place, went to meet them. Keir was taking the tall blonde's coat, and mercifully missed the expression of amusement which crossed her face as she saw them together. Jennifer was almost a perfect replica of Angela in both colouring and stature, and just for a moment Mickey wondered if he never got tired of the same unvaried combination, never yearned for a redhead or brunette to enliven his diet.

Still, his taste in women had little to do with her, and, stepping forwards, she pinned a polite smile to her lips as she murmured quietly, 'Good evening.'

'Miss James. Oh, I'm so pleased to meet you.'

The warmth in the blonde's voice startled Mickey for a moment, and she shot a quick look in Keir's direction for explanation.

135

'I've just told Jennifer about her "surprise", and it turns out she's probably one of your greatest fans. She's been singing me your praises all the way up here in the lift.'

There was a dryness to his tone which was unmistakable, at least to Mickey, and she had to stifle a small laugh as she realised just how much it must have stuck in his throat to admit there was somebody in the world who found her more than just a prying busybody and nuisance. Stepping forwards, she held her hand out to Jennifer Lancaster in a greeting which was far warmer than she had ever intended.

'I'm delighted to meet you, Miss Lancaster.'

'Oh, please call me Jennifer,' the girl replied quickly, taking her hand in a firm clasp.

Close to she was even more beautiful than Mickey had at first realised, with a honey-tinted skin and soft blue eyes which held only warmth and, mercifully, none of Angela's veiled hostility.

'I just can't tell you how thrilled I was when Keir told me what he'd arranged. However did he manage to get you to agree to it?'

'He can be very persuasive when he chooses,' Mickey replied quietly, irony lacing her tone, an irony she knew wasn't lost on the man standing listening.

'Oh, but can't he?' Jennifer replied with a soft laugh. 'It's just part of his charm, don't you find?'

'Mmmm, I suppose you could say that,' she replied more tartly. Charm, indeed! As far as she was concerned, the man had as much charm as a rattlesnake, and was probably far more deadly! However, now was not the time to dwell on all his bad points, it would take far too long to begin to list them. Turning aside, she murmured politely, 'Well, I'll leave you to get settled in, then, Jennifer, while I get on with the dinner. I thought we'd make a start tomorrow on those lessons, just before lunch.'

'Oh, do we have to wait so long? Honestly, Mickey, it just seems sacrilege to have you here and waste all these hours. Why don't I give you a hand straight away now?'

'Well . . .' Nonplussed, Mickey looked towards Keir for

guidance, but his set expression gave little away. With a mental shrug she decided to agree. If he didn't like it, then it was his problem, wasn't it?

'Of course you can help if you want to, Jennifer, but I must warn you that I've not planned anything elaborate for tonight. Come along to the kitchen when you're ready.'

'Oh, I'll come now.'

Pushing up the sleeves of her expensive knitted dress, Jennifer led the way towards the kitchen, pausing to murmur a belated, 'You don't mind, do you, darling?' to Keir, who was standing silently listening to their exchange.

'No, of course not. Enjoy yourself,' he replied, and something in his voice made Mickey turn so that for a moment their eyes met. He should have been pleased that they were getting on so well, surely? After all, the sooner she found someone suitable for him, the sooner he'd be free of her and she of him. So why was it she was certain it was sorrow, not happiness lurking in that blue gaze? It worried her, made her hurry quickly down the passage to the kitchen, somehow strangely afraid to linger and maybe find the answer.

'That's lovely, Jennifer, perfectly cooked. Now, if you'll just flake the fish into biggish pieces, and take out all the bones, then we're nearly ready.'

The two women had worked steadily together for the best part of an hour and, as Mickey's previous feeling of unease had settled, she'd found herself impressed by both Jennifer's ability and enthusiasm, and had gone out of her way to teach her a few special tricks which would turn a rather simple meal into something special. This sauce for the fish was one of them: a delicate blend of fresh cream, eggs and butter, with a hint of piquant herbs to save it from being just too overpoweringly rich and creamy. She carefully lifted the heavy pan from the heat and stirred the sauce gently, making sure that it didn't get any chance to curdle or separate, as it could do if the cook was unwary.

Jennifer had the fish neatly flaked on to a large,

attractive dish for serving, and at Mickey's instruction poured the sauce over it, then finished it with a delicate lacy garnish of fresh parsley.

'That's lovely. I'll carry it through, shall I?' Lifting up the dish, Jennifer walked swiftly through to the dining-room and put it down on the table, stopping as she made a swift mental count of the place settings. There was a tiny frown of puzzlement creasing her smooth brow as she turned to Mickey, who had followed with a heaped bowl of salad and a platter of hot, fragrant rolls.

'Why are there only two places set, Mickey? Are you going out?'

'Why, no, but I thought you'd want to be by yourselves.'

'Oh, rubbish! There's no way I'm having you eating in the kitchen on your own while we're in here. Don't be ridiculous! You must eat with us . . . mustn't she, Keir?'

Jennifer shot a swift look over Mickey's shoulder at the tall man who was standing just inside the doorway, listening.

'Of course she must,' he murmured, and Mickey wondered if only she could hear the faint thread of mockery in his tone. However, there was no way she was going to accept the invitation; it was one thing to play teacher, but quite another to play gooseberry.

Lifting her head, she stared determinedly back at him as she replied, 'Thank you, but really I'd prefer not to join you. I'm sure you must have things you want to discuss by yourselves.'

'It's no good arguing, we won't take no for an answer, will we, darling? Now, sit down while I get another place laid. Is everything in the kitchen?'

'I . . . I . . . yes, in the cupboards over the fridge.'

There was little else she could do, short of causing a scene, so with marked ill grace she sat stiffly down and spread the napkin carefully across the skirt of her green linen dress, aware that Keir had already taken the seat opposite. Looking up, she shot him a brief glance of apology before murmuring quietly, 'I'm sorry, I didn't mean to intrude on . . .'

'Forget it, Mickey. It doesn't matter.'

Reaching over, Keir helped himself from the dishes, and with a mental shrug Mickey decided to follow his lead and not let this change of plans upset her. Taking a hot roll from the basket, she broke it deftly with her fingers, smiling as a sudden thought struck her.

'What's so funny?'

The low question brought her attention back to the man seated opposite, and she looked up at him, her lips still softly curved with a lingering amusement.

'I was just wondering what Angela would think if she could see the hired help sitting down at the table.'

His expression had softened as he'd studied her smiling face, but now it hardened at the memory of his other far more troublesome guest.

'Frankly, what Angela thinks doesn't bother me.'

'So she's off your list, then?'

'She was off my list the moment she hit you, Mickey. Right off.'

'So my score didn't influence your decision, then?'

'To write her off? No, it didn't. Frankly, it only agreed with what I'd revised mine to, though perhaps I hadn't gotten around to writing it down so succinctly,' he replied, his tone lightening as he remembered her red-penned 'zero'. 'Mind you, Mickey, if you could just leave me a discreet note next time, I'd be just as happy.'

'Of course. Actually I had intended to leave a note on your desk before I left that morning, but when I went into the study Angela was there, so I left it taped to the fridge instead.'

'Angela was in my study doing what?' Puzzlement laced his voice, but Mickey couldn't satisfy it.

'I don't know exactly. She said something about ringing for a taxi, but I didn't hear her using the phone.'

'That's strange, she knew I'd arranged to take her home.' For a moment a hint of unease crossed his face, before he quickly pushed it aside as Jennifer entered.

'Right, I think I've got everything. How's the fish?'

Swiftly Jennifer laid another place at the table, before sitting down and helping herself from the dish.

'Delicious. You're quite a cook, Mickey,' Keir said.

The compliment was quite obviously sincere, and Mickey felt a quick surge of pleasure flood through her as she heard it. However, an innate honesty refused to let her take all the glory and, smiling, she said, 'Actually, Jennifer did most of it.'

'Rubbish! All I did was follow your instructions, Mickey. Honestly, Keir, she makes everything sound so simple, I'm sure even you could turn out a decent meal; you'll have to get her to give you lessons.'

'Mmm, that sounds like an interesting idea. How about it, then, Mickey? Do you think I'd make a good pupil? What sort of score would you give me?'

Mickey caught his gaze across the table, and suddenly knew that cooking was the very last thing he had on his mind. There was an instant's brief, intense silence when the room seemed to shiver out of focus and fade slowly away, leaving them locked in the middle of some private, silent conversation.

A silent gasp of pain broke the silence, and Mickey shot a glance at the other girl, quickly taking in the streaming eyes and convulsive choking movements of her throat.

'Quick, Keir, get some water. She's got something stuck in her throat.' She hurried round the table and laid a soothing hand on the blonde girl's shoulder.

'It's a bone, a fish bone.' Poor Jennifer could hardly force the words out through her pain-numbed throat, speaking in a low whisper which Mickey, bending over her, could just hear.

'What is it?'

Dripping glass in hand, Keir hurried back into the room, kneeling down besides Jennifer's chair to offer it to her.

'A fish bone,' Mickey answered for her.

'A fish bone! Dammit, woman, don't you know better than to be so careless and leave bones in when you cook a meal!' Anxiety made his voice harsh and furious as he gazed up at her, but she didn't try to argue or explain that Jennifer had prepared the fish for the table. Her main concern at the moment was to give the other girl some relief from the pain, so she ignored him totally as she bent towards her.

'Just sip this water, slowly. See if it will dislodge the bone.'

Holding the ice-cold glass to her lips, she watched as Jennifer sipped and painfully tried to swallow, but it was obvious from the fresh tears which sprang immediately to the soft blue eyes that the remedy was meeting with no success. Although Jennifer's first understandable wave of panic had subsided, she was still distressed and obviously in pain. Looking up at Keir with eyes which only mirrored his concern, Mickey made an instant decision.

'Will you get your car? I think you'd better take her to the hospital. There's no point in taking a chance on that bone getting deeply embedded.'

'Of course, I think that's best, too.'

His previous anger had faded, but his eyes were still icy when they focused on Mickey's anxious face. She knew he blamed her for the accident, but let him; he always blamed her anyway, so it was hardly something new and strange.

'Oh, no, really . . .' Jennifer's low croaked protest did more to convince them she needed to go than that she didn't, and Mickey shushed her soothingly before hurrying from the room in Keir's wake to fetch her coat. Within minutes she had Jennifer snugly bundled into the cream cashmere jacket and in the lift down to the foyer where Keir was waiting. Between them they led her out to the car and got her comfortably seated. Striding quickly round, Keir stopped beside the driver's door, his expression grim as he faced Mickey.

'Wait here. I'll speak to you later.'

No please, no thank you, just that brief command, then he was gone in a spurt of gravel which stung at her legs as she stood on the steps, watching.

How dared he, how dared he order her around like a lackey? She'd wait all right, if only to tell him exactly what

she thought of him and his orders, and she flounced back
inside the building and up to the flat, kicking the front
door with her heel to close it.

If he'd asked her now what was his score—oh, boy,
would she tell him! It would probably make even zero look
healthy!

With a low groan Mickey awoke and, raising her hand,
eased the stiffened muscles in her neck and shoulder as
they screamed in protest at her attempts to move. The
room was dark and, forcing herself into a sitting position,
she snapped on a nearby lamp, glad even of its soft light to
dispel the gloom.

Her skin felt cool, chilly, despite the fact she'd changed
into a long velour robe before she'd started to keep this
vigil, and she rubbed her hands briskly up and down her
arms to restore some warmth to her circulation. What she
needed was a nice, hot, strong cup of tea to revive both her
and her waning anger, ready for that damned American's
return, which, judging by the lateness of the hour, must be
soon.

Standing up, she took a step towards the door, but
stopped as she heard the faint but unmistakable sound of
voices coming from the hall, and realised that was what
must have wakened her from her doze. They must be
back, Jennifer must be all right, and with a feeling of relief
she hurried forwards as fast as her poor cramped limbs
would let her to greet them, or at least to greet Jennifer.
What she had in mind to say to Mr Keir Grant was
something far less pleasant.

The door swung open and Mickey had one startled
moment to wonder why they hadn't switched on the hall
lights, before suddenly everything started to happen and
she found herself, though now awake, thrust back into a
nightmare situation.

'Who's she?'

'God knows, but don't just stand there, grab her before
she screams!'

Two voices, two figures, two darker patches against a

dark background . . . two complete and total strangers, and Mickey took a few steps backwards, feeling behind her for some solid support as the first weakening shivers of terror crawled up her skin like cold, dead fingers.

'Oh, no, you don't. Get her, Terry, she's after the phone!'

One of the figures lunged towards her, grasping her arms in vicious hold which shot pain right through her, and she let out a soft moan of protest.

'Let me go.'

Quickly, she tried to wrench her arms free from the man's cruel hold, but he wouldn't let her, tightening his grip till she felt she must scream with the pain he was inflicting. Forcing her backwards, he pushed her roughly down on to the sofa before tearing the phone from its socket and hurling it across the room with a clatter which made her flinch deeper into the cushions for protection.

'What are we going to do?'

The voice was young, frightened and, turning her gaze up to him, Mickey realised with a sudden start that despite his size and strength he was little more than a boy.

'We're going to do exactly as we planned, that's what—except now we'll have a little more fun, won't we, darling?'

And Mickey's stomach lurched sickeningly as she swiftly grasped his meaning. With eyes widened with horror she watched as the second man advanced and sat down on the sofa next to her, so close she could feel the heat, smell the rank, unclean odour of his body. Swiftly her eyes skittered over his face, searching desperately for some sign that might give her hope he didn't mean what he'd implied, but it was blank except for the glitter burning in his hard eyes as he watched her like a terrier might watch a rabbit, and she knew with a dreadful clarity that there would be nothing she could offer which would deter him from what he was planning.

But she had to try, had to do something, had to give her fear-numbed brain time to function and find some way of escaping.

'What do you want?' Her voice was so strained that for a moment she hardly recognised it as her own.

'Want? Well, not much, darling. A little money, a little jewellery . . . a little fun.' Leaning forwards, he flicked at the top buttons of her robe, pushing them open, his eyes sweeping over the exposed 'V' of creamy skin with an expression which made her skin crawl with horror. Quickly, desperately, she raised her hands and tried to fasten it again, but with a deceptively slow and easy movement he reached forwards and tore the rest of the front open to expose the full swell of her breasts, thinly covered by the lacy cups of her bra.

Opening her mouth, Mickey started to scream, but barely a whisper of sound escaped before he clamped a hand over her lips. Bending his head, he stated in a voice which was even more frightening for its softness, 'You scream now, darling, and it'll be the last sound you'll ever make.'

Then there was the cold feel of something hard and smooth sliding against the soft skin of her throat, and when he released her she saw he held a knife, and every single nerve in her body began to quake and tremble in fear.

'Now then, Terry, you go and see what you can find, while this young lady and I get better acquainted,' he ordered briefly, never lifting his eyes from the sight of her soft, exposed flesh. Mickey had to force herself not to move, not to snatch the torn edges of the robe together, not to startle him into using that thin, sharp edge of steel.

'But . . .'

'Do it! And take your time, son—don't hurry.'

The younger man strode reluctantly from the room, and Mickey felt her heart sink even further as she watched him leave. Now there was no one except her and this monster, and in the briefest, clearest flash realised she'd almost prefer it if he knifed her rather than what he so obviously planned. If only she could think of something to divert him, do something, but it was impossible while her mind as well as her body felt as though it was caught in some gigantic spider's web of horror.

He shifted towards her, the cruel, shining blade of the knife resting deceptively gently against her cheek as he slid one hand inside the torn neck of her robe and grasped roughly at her breast, and a slow river of desperate tears slid down her face at this defiling touch on her body.

'Mickey! What the hell are you doing with the door open?'

Keir stood in the doorway, his face hard, eyes blazing with irritated impatience, then in one swift, all-encompassing glance he took in the scene: her tears, her terror, the man's hands on her body, the knife, and a look of such total and savage fury contorted his face that even Mickey flinched.

'Let her go.' His voice was low, black ice cutting through the grey stillness in the room, and she felt, sensed the man hesitate, so great was the force of power behind the command. Then there was a swift blur of movement in the hall, the shape of the boy, black-silhouetted against the glare of the lit chandeliers, and Mickey suddenly found all the courage she'd lost before speeding back to her so she could shout a warning.

'Keir! Look out!'

Inistinctively he sidestepped, avoiding the blow which had been aimed at his head, but staggering to his knees as it caught him across the shoulder. The boy drew back his foot to kick him as he lay there stunned, and in that instant, that tiny flicker of time, the web clinging round Mickey snapped. Knocking the man's hand away from her face, she jumped up and raced across the room and with a sharp twist spun the boy off his feet and hurled him back out into the hallway, to crash against the wall with a jolting thud which knocked the breath and the sense from his body.

'My God, woman, what are you?' Kneeling, Keir looked up at her in amazement, as much stunned by the fluid beauty of the throw as by the recent blow he'd received. She grinned down at him, blood once more racing warmly through her veins.

'A black belt at judo . . . I've just remembered.'

There was a sudden movement across the room, and both looked towards their other uninvited guest, who was now standing, the knife clutched desperately before him. Slowly Keir straightened, flexing the aching muscles in his shoulder, stretching like a big cat about to spring.

'Yours or mine?' Mickey asked politely, not taking her eyes from the man who was looking far less frightening now Keir was here.

'Oh, mine, please, definitely mine.'

There was a note of sheer hatred in his deep, dark voice which told her more of what he was feeling than a thousand words could have done. Standing back, she watched calmly as he advanced, backing the man into the corner.

There was a flurry of movement, a few familiar grunts and oaths uttered in an American accent, then the satisfying, sickening sound of bone connecting with bone, followed by silence, and Mickey hardly dared check who was the victor.

Footsteps crossed the room towards her and, raising her head, she stared dumbly up into a pair of achingly familiar blue eyes . . . then quietly fainted.

CHAPTER ELEVEN

'AND she'll be all right, you're certain?'

'Absolutely, Mr Grant, she's just shocked, that's all. There's no physical damage done. From what you told me, you got here just in time to save her from . . . well, to stop the incident from going any further.'

And Keir felt his jaw clench at this reminder of what could have happened if he'd arrived even minutes later.

'Well, I'll be off downstairs, then, and take another look at the night porter. He was lucky, too . . . if you can call a crack on the head which knocked him out cold "lucky"! But still, let's face it, with two of them to contend with when he opened the doors, there was little he could do, and he could have fared worse. Did the police say what they were after, by the way?'

Keir gave a shrug, impatient for him to go, and answered briefly, 'Cash, credit cards, jewellery . . . just the usual.'

'Mmm, I see.' Sensing he'd almost outstayed his welcome, the doctor walked towards the door, pausing to add a final word. 'Now don't forget, give me a ring if you think she needs me again, but I've given her something to make her sleep, so she should be all right.'

'Of course, thank you, Doctor.'

Keir let him out, then closed the door slowly, pushing it firmly back into place. There'd been no sign of a forced entry into the flat, so it looked as if Mickey had failed to close the door properly when she'd come back upstairs, and just for a moment he cursed himself for not having the lock changed earlier. But still, it was too late now, more a case of bolting the stable door after the horse had fled really, and no amount of recriminations would alter what had happened.

It could have been worse, a lot worse, the police had

147

stated firmly, and Keir knew they were right, but somehow
it was little comfort to realise it when all he had to do was
close his eyes for a series of haunting images to overwhelm
him: Mickey, face wet with tears, twisted with terror, and
that man holding a knife to her throat while his hand
roamed over her body. Turning, he smote his fist against
the door in a savage fury, wanting to crush those images
for ever.

'Keir?'

Mickey's voice calling from the bedroom held more
than a trace of remembered terror, and Keir silently cursed
himself for frightening her again.

'It's all right, honey, I'm here.'

Quickly he strode along the passage and, turning the
handle, strove to get a grip on his emotions before he
entered the room. Mickey was propped against a mound
of pillows, her dark hair curling wildly around her
alabaster-pale face. Her eyes were huge, shadowed, tainted
with the lingering memory of the attack, and Keir felt an
overwhelming desire to pull her to him and wipe that
memory from her mind for ever.

'Have they all gone?' she asked quietly and calmly, too
calmly, he thought, watching her face.

'Yes.'

Walking forwards, he ran his eyes over her face in
concern. This calm wasn't natural, more the result of
shock. It worried him.

'I suppose the police will be back in the morning.'

'Yes, they want you to make a statement, I'm afraid.'

'Yes, I heard,' she answered flatly.

Even through the closed door of her bedroom, Mickey
had heard Keir's roar of fury and refusal to let the police
interview her that night. He'd been downright rude in his
protection of her, and she'd been immeasurably grateful.
There was no way she wanted to go over the details at the
moment, not until she'd managed to set some distance
between herself and these feelings of shame and horror
which filled her. She desperately searched for something to
say which would keep the questions at bay a while longer.

'How is Jennifer? Did they manage to get the bone out?' Her voice was low, strained, still tinged with recent horror and, hearing it, Keir knew his questions and her answers would have to wait, at least for the moment. There was no way he wanted to upset her further tonight, after all she'd gone through.

'She's fine, or will be after a good night's sleep. Luckily the bone wasn't too deeply embedded, so it wasn't too difficult to get out, though I doubt if she will feel up to singing in the bath for a few days.'

'No, I'm sure she won't.' With an effort Mickey mustered up a small, thin smile, her eyes meeting his across the width of the room before sliding quickly away, missing the expression which crossed his face. He hated to see her looking so tense and nervous, but knew there was little he could do right at the moment except follow her lead and keep the conversational ball rolling.

'She also explained that I'd been quite wrong to blame you for the accident, that she, in fact, had prepared the fish for the table, so it seems I owe you an apology, Mickey.'

'It doesn't matter,' she murmured softly. So much had happened in these past few hours that it had put the previous incident and his unjust anger very much in the shade. Still, it had been nice of Jennifer to bother, to care enough to see she wasn't blamed. She said sincerely, 'She's a nice girl, Keir. I liked her very much. Oh, I know I'm hardly qualified to make a judgement on such a short meeting, but I found her very pleasant, as well as beautiful. I'm sure you'd have to go a long way to find anyone else who is so obviously suitable as Jennifer Lancaster.'

'Yes, I'm sure you're right,' he answered levelly, meeting her gaze, and Mickey wondered why his agreement should suddenly cause her so much pain. Jennifer was everything he wanted: cool, beautiful, poised, kind and friendly . . . the perfect choice to be his wife. Finding her should be the answer to all her hopes and dreams of putting an end to this strange agreement which tied her

and Keir Grant together. But somehow, strangely, it was
pain which curled and twisted through her heart, not
pleasure, and she looked away hurriedly before he could
read it in her face, but she was too slow.

'What is it, Mickey? Are you all right?' Moving further
into the room, Keir sat down on the edge of the bed and
studied her intently. 'Are you quite sure that you're not
hurt anywhere? That man didn't . . . didn't . . .'

'No, honestly, I'm fine,' she answered quickly. There
was no way she could explain that sudden vivid flash of
pain to him, no way at all.

'Are you sure?' Reaching forwards, Keir took her cold,
nervous hands in his and chafed them gently.

'Yes,' she whispered.

Now that he was so close and watching her so intently,
Mickey felt herself unable to meet his gaze, and looked
down, staring at their hands linked on the soft green
coverlet of the bed, his so big and tanned, hers so small
and pale. A huge great knot of anguish seemed to be
building up inside her, as though one pain had opened the
floodgates for another, had broken down the mental dam
which had held the memories of the attack at bay. She
fought desperately to hang on to her control.

'Mickey.'

'Yes?' She could barely answer, her voice a thin thread
of choked sound which hardly reached his ears.

'Mickey, look at me, honey,' he prompted gently.

'I can't.'

'Why not?'

There was a minute's long, long silence while she fought
to make some sense of the emotions which were writhing
snake-like round her brain and give him an answer he
could maybe understand.

'I . . . I . . . oh, Keir! I feel so used, so dirty, so shamed!'

The words sobbed from her, and with a low groan Keir
pulled her to him, wrapping her tight in his arms and
rocking her gently against his body as he tried to absorb
her pain.

She cried for a long time, deep, silent sobs which shook

her slender body, and all the time he held her, saying nothing, just held her. Then slowly, gradually, the sobs slackened and, lifting his hand, Keir ran it gently over her tangled hair, smoothing it away from her hot, flushed cheeks. With a start Mickey felt him tremble, felt the shudders which racked his big frame.

'Keir,' she whispered, 'what is it?'

'What is it? Oh, God, Mickey, when I saw him with you, so help me, I wanted to kill him for touching you.'

The words were wrenched from him, and as Mickey looked up it was as though suddenly all the layers, all the armour, had fallen away, leaving him strangely vulnerable. She locked her arms around him and held him to her; her turn to be the comforter and his the comforted, her turn to absorb his pain.

The thought gave her strength, gave her the courage to do something she knew would be courting trouble given the highly emotional state they were both in. But nothing, nothing mattered except he was here and hurting and, turning her head, she pressed her lips to his and kissed him.

His response was instant, spontaneous, a deep surge of feeling which welled through him with a force he couldn't control. She kissed him and he kissed her back, lips and tongues moving in a perfect harmony which fired their blood. Gently he eased her back against the mound of pillows while he rained a shower of burning kisses over her cheeks, her chin, her eyes, her hair, as though he couldn't bear to leave any tiny inch of her unkissed. His hands trailed round the delicate curve of her ears and down her throat, across the fragile bones of her shoulders, and Mickey felt herself burning with the heat which was building deep inside her. Everywhere he touched with lips or hands she burned, ached for more, and she arched towards him shamelessly, pressing her body closer and closer against the hardness of his.

Then suddenly, strangely the sensations began to fade, swept away by a deep languor which stole over her, making her arms, her head, her body heavy, as though she was trying to swim through deep, deep water. She could still feel and taste the kisses he was trailing over her hot skin, but somehow she found it impossible to respond, impossible to keep her sleepy eyes open.

'Mickey, honey, what is it?' Feeling the limpness of her body, Keir shot upright, alarm racing through him, making him feel as breathless from worry as from passion. 'Sweetheart, wake up. Are you all right? Mickey, speak to me, dammit!'

Gathering her to him, he pressed her head gently back against his shoulder while he stared down at her drooping lids, utterly astounded that his kisses could cause this sort of reaction.

Forcing her heavy eyelids open, Mickey stared up at him, kiss-swollen lips faintly curved into a sleepy smile.

'I'm sorry, I just can't keep my eyes open. It must be the tablets the doctor gave me. I'm so sorry,' she mumbled, before her eyes drifted closed once more.

Looking down at her peaceful face, Keir gave a quiet chuckle as he wryly acknowledged it would need a few hours before he could wake this Sleeping Beauty with a kiss.

Hours later, with a pearly light drifting through the uncurtained windows, Mickey awoke, feeling strangely content, warm and cared for. The few hours' sleep had done her good, allowed her overcharged emotions to settle and place the attack in its proper perspective. True, she'd been handled in a way that had never happened to her before, but none of it had been her fault, she was not to blame, and now she refused to feel ashamed.

Stretching catlike under the warm covers, her body brushed lightly against something and she froze, her heart leaping in her chest with a mighty lurch. Slowly, carefully her hand slid sideways in an exploring foray which her eyes didn't dare to make, and was swiftly captured in a warm, familiar grasp.

'Good morning.'

Keir's deep, beautiful voice rumbled softly across the

mound of pillows and, turning her head, she stared into
his blue eyes, wondering why it felt so right to find him
lying there beside her.

'Good morning.'

For a moment they both just looked at each other, and
Mickey felt the first trace of colour bloom in her cheeks at
his expression. He was watching her with such longing,
such tenderness and caring that it stole what little was left
of her breath.

Reaching out, he ran a long, tanned finger gently down
the softness of her cheek, before tracing it lightly round
the curved bow of her lips. Mickey felt her heart begin to
hammer, felt the blood start to surge once more through
her veins like molten lava.

'Do you remember what we were doing last night before
you fell asleep?' he asked softly.

'Yes,' she whispered, somehow afraid that if she spoke
too loudly she might break the spell and he'd disappear.

'Well, I've made it one of my strictest policies, Miss
James, never to leave any business unfinished.'

'Have you? Well, I think that's the right idea.'

'Good.' Leaning towards her he stopped as a sudden
thought struck him and he smiled. 'Do you know, that's
probably the first time in our whole relationship that
you've ever agreed with me.'

'Is it?' Moving slightly, she edged herself closer, feeling
the way his muscles flinched and flickered as she settled
herself against him. Raising her hand, she stroked it slowly
down the side of his face, loving the soft but harsh feel of
his beard brush against the warm skin of her palm.
'Perhaps, Mr Grant, you should try a different type of
question.'

'Mmm, you think so?' Turning his head, he nipped
gently at the soft inner flesh of her hand, feeling the quick,
unhidden shudder which passed through her at his touch.
'Well, Miss James, how about this one. May I kiss you?'

'Yes, please.' And, reaching up, she linked her fingers in
the cool silky hair at the nape of his neck and pulled his
head down towards her, suddenly impatient for his kiss.

His lips slid over hers, lightly, gently at first, tracing their outline with the warm tip of his tongue till Mickey felt she would explode with longing. Then, swiftly, the kiss hardened, deepened, till he was kissing her with a blatant, disturbing passion which sent tremors coursing through her, in echo of the previous night's passion.

His hands ran down her body, teasing, tormenting, stroking over her heated skin and arousing her to a fervour of mindless longing which had her clinging to him. Then he gently slid the thin straps of her gown off her shoulders, and for a moment stared down at the soft curves of her breasts, all creamy-pale and rose-tipped in the gentle early morning light.

'You're beautiful, so beautiful,' he murmured quietly, a broken timbre to his deep, soft voice. Then, dipping his head, he kissed first one breast then the other, tongue, lips and teeth teasing at the hardened nipples in a rhythm which sent fire curling through her. Twisting her head against the pillows, she murmured his name over and over in an agony of wanting. Raising her hands, she ran them lightly down the strong slope of his back, feeling the muscles bunch and quiver at her touch, urging him closer, closer.

Then everything was movement, touch, sensation; skin against skin, flesh against flesh, until that moment when they must become one and she felt him hesitate, pause as he realised this was the first time she had ever given herself to a man.

'Mickey?'

Grasping at the very last of his control, Keir looked down into her eyes, somehow unable to find the words to voice his question. Raising her hips to bring them into closer contact with his, she gave him the answer. There was a moment's brief, unexpected stab of pain which made her muscles clench and tighten, then slowly it began to recede, pushed aside by some other far deeper, more demanding sensation which refused to be denied. Clinging to him, their bodies locked in this act of loving, she found herself caught up by the need to climb that peak of ecstasy he was leading her to. Then, with a little cry of half-disbelief, she reached it and felt herself tumble through a star-spangled darkness of joy.

Later, looking down at his head pressed into the curve of her shoulder, she knew there was no longer any way she could deny what she was feeling, knew that no amount of showers or reasoning could change the one simple fact . . . she loved him, now and for ever. Loved her tough American blackmailer!

Seated behind his desk, Keir looked quietly down at the array of prints spread across its polished mahogany surface. Slowly, carefully, his gaze slid from one glossy black and white rectangle to the next, studying the two figures locked in the passionate embrace, and felt his stomach tighten in a swift, spiralling curl of longing. Despite the long hours he and Mickey had spent making love, he was still filled by a burning hunger, an insatiable desire to possess her delicious creamy body yet again; scooping the pile of prints together, he slid them quickly back into their packet to end the torment, pausing as a thought struck him.

For several moments he stared down at the plain fold of manila paper, then gently slid one print back out and slipped it into the bottom drawer of the desk. Picking up the rest of the packet, he strode from the room and made his way along to the kitchen, where Mickey was humming tunelessly as she washed some dishes. Skimming the envelope on to the table, he walked up quietly and, wrapping his arms tight around her middle, drew her back against his body.

'Oh!'

Startled, Mickey stiffened briefly, then, feeling the familiar brush of his beard against the smooth skin of her cheek, she relaxed, letting her slight weight settle against him. Turning her head, she pressed a swift kiss to the side of his neck, loving the way his pulse leapt in instant appreciation of the gesture.

'How long are you going to be?' he asked quietly.

'Only a few minutes . . . why?'

'Well, it seems a waste to have you here and let you spend all the time in the kitchen. Frankly I can think of a few better things to do than dishes,' he murmured wickedly, bending his head to nibble at the cords of her neck, and chuckling slightly as he felt her responsive shudder.

'You, Keir Grant, have a one-track mind at the moment, do you know that?'

'Mmmm . . .' Gently he trailed a line of kisses up her neck to the soft curve of her jawline, and Mickey felt her knees begin to weaken at his touch.

'Keir, stop it,' she scolded, trying desperately to cling hold to at least some shred of common sense while she still had the strength to do so.

'Why should I? It's been ages since I kissed you, with the police being here all the damned morning. I think I deserve a reward for my patience.'

Spinning her round, he grasped her firmly by the shoulders, the gleam in his eyes stating blatantly that all that patience had now disappeared. But, raising her hands against the strong muscles of his chest, Mickey held him off, knowing that once he kissed her she'd never find enough will-power to say all the things which must be said. The shift in their relationship had been so unexpected, so sudden, she still felt shell-shocked; one minute she was a twenty-five-year-old virgin, the next his lover, and frankly it was a lot to contend with. Not that she regretted what she'd done for one moment; how could she possibly regret something which had felt so right, been so perfect and given them both so much pleasure? But there was still a lot between them, a lot of very stale air which needed clearing.

Reaching up on tiptoe, she pressed a swift kiss to his warm lips, then moved swiftly out of his grasp before she gave in to the almost overwhelming urge to linger. Walking across the room, she sat down at the far side of the table, staring down at her hands as she tried to find the words to explain her feelings and ask her questions, even though, deep down, she dreaded the answers.

'What's the matter, honey?'

Leaning a hip against the counter, Keir studied her quietly.

'Keir . . . look, all this has been so sudden, so unexpected that I . . .'

'You regret it, wish it hadn't happened?'

Ice was overlaying his deep tones, frosting the warmth from his blue eyes and hastily she reassured him.

'No, that's one thing I don't . . . I don't regret one minute of it.' Looking up, she stared intently back at him, willing him to see the sincerity in her eyes. The very last thing she wanted to do was damage this new precious feeling between them with some silly misunderstanding.

'I'm glad.'

Crossing the room, he pulled out a chair and sat opposite her, linking his long fingers with hers on the top of the table.

'Just tell me what it is that's troubling you, then, Mickey,' he said softly, and the gentleness in his tone gave her the courage she needed to continue.

'I want to know where we go from here. If this was just one of those things that happen, if it really didn't mean anything, then I want you to tell me now.'

There was a tormented look to her soft hazel eyes which cut into him like a razor and, leaning forwards, he pressed a warm kiss of reassurance to her stiff lips before saying quietly. 'Mickey, I'm not good with words, not good at coping with feelings, but what I can tell you is that what we shared was the best, most beautiful thing that ever happened to me, and I don't want to lose it.'

'You don't?'

'No. You're not just a one-night stand, Mickey. You're far too special. I know we started off badly, but I want you to try and forget all that if you can. I think these might help. Here.'

Slithering the envelope across the table, Keir placed her hand gently down on top of it, covering it with his own before saying quietly, 'I want you to have these photographs . . . I no longer need them.'

And, looking down at the plain buff packet, Mickey felt her eyes swim with tears of joy and happiness at this evidence of how much his feelings had changed towards her. Now he no longer saw her as a threat, but as someone he could trust, and maybe, just maybe, in the not too dim and distant future that trust would turn into the one thing she yearned for most . . . love.

The rest of the day passed in a haze of quiet pleasure and happiness which Mickey knew would stay in her heart for ever. Keir was attentive, refusing to let her do too much which might tire her, and Mickey, used to coping on her own, suddenly found out just how good it could be to feel so cherished.

Curled up on the long, soft sofa in the lounge, they whiled away the afternoon watching an old Cary Grant movie on the television, each surprised and strangely pleased that the other should share this taste for rather less than intellectual viewing. Head resting in the hollow of his shoulder, body warmed by his, Mickey enjoyed the simple pleasure of them just being together.

For over an hour they laughed at the glib story-line, the witty comments, but then didn't even realise they'd missed the ending when one of their soft shared kisses flared into a sudden, startling passion. Side by side on the sofa, the light from the television flickering in a dreamlike kaleidoscope of patterns over their now bare skin, they made love: slowly, gently, but with a deep intensity which brought soft tears to Mickey's eyes, blurring her vision so that all she could focus on was Keir watching her with a hunger in his eyes she ached to fill. He was everything to her now—her heart, her soul, her very being—and she told him, not in the words some instinct warned her it was too soon for, but in her response, in her unstinted giving of herself, and watched as the hunger in him was slowly filled.

Later, held close in his arms, skin still damply pressed against skin, Mickey looked up into his eyes and said softly, 'I never knew it could be like this, Keir, never.'

There was wonder in her voice and, dipping his head, Keir kissed her gently before saying quietly, 'It's never been like this before, either, Mickey.'

'It hasn't?'

Startled, Mickey stared up at him for a silent moment. 'But surely you've . . . well, you've . . .' Hot colour flooded her cheeks, and he chuckled, running a soothing finger over the rose-tinted skin. 'Oh, yes, I definitely have, but never like this before. Never with a woman who could give so generously of herself as you do, honey. What we just shared was something rare, something so very special I can hardly believe that it was real.'

'But it was real, Keir.'

Raising her hand, she ran it down the curve of his cheek and across the hard bones of his shoulder in a gentle caress, strangely moved by what he'd said. Lifting her closer against the strong planes of his body, Keir held her to him for a few seconds.

'Oh, yes, it was real, all right, very real and very special . . . just like you.'

That night, lying next to Keir in his bed, having given in to his refusal to let her return home with a quite uncharacteristic ease which had set them both laughing, Mickey looked down at his sleeping form and knew that she would give everything she possessed just to have him keep that feeling. For him, she would always want to be the one and only special woman in his life!

CHAPTER TWELVE

SOFT lights, sweet music and the man she loved . . . what more could any girl ask for? Not a lot, except perhaps another ten minutes to let the dream reach its perfect conclusion.

Groaning, Mickey rolled over and, slamming a hand on the radio button, cut off the gravelly voice which bore little resemblance to the rich, deep tones which had filled her dreams. She'd done a very late dinner party the night before, on top of two demonstrations and yet another photo session to finish off the insert, and quite frankly she was feeling shattered. But still, there was compensation for getting up at such a disgusting hour, and it came in such an attractive six-foot package! Keir was collecting her at nine that morning, and if she didn't get a move on then she'd never be ready. Tossing back the covers, she jumped out of bed and made her way along to the bathroom.

Twenty minutes later, showered, dressed and marginally less sleepy, she was down in the kitchen and, plugging in the kettle, waited for it to boil while she let her mind drift over the past week; seven short days which seemed to have changed her life for ever. So much had happened in this one short week that at times she had to pinch herself to know she wasn't dreaming, to know that she hadn't imagined the way their relationship had shifted from antagonism to passion at such a breathtaking, heart-stopping speed.

But no, it was no dream. She had only to close her eyes for a hundred images of Keir to appear, a hundred fleeting impressions too real to have been imagined. Keir laughing as he ran with her through the rain-soaked park to shelter under a spread of trees and kiss, damp lips clinging warmly together; Keir bending towards her, face serious, intent, as he explained some part of the deal he was negotiating; Keir pulling her to him, their bodies brushing gently as they drifted to the slow strains of a waltz one evening; Keir loving her in all those tender gestures, all those little ways except the words she ached to hear. If only he would just say he loved her, tell her what he planned, what he intended to happen in their relationship, then she would feel so much easier. For her, it was all so clear-cut and simple; she loved him more than she could have imagined it possible to love anyone, and wanted desperately to spend the rest of her life with him as his wife. But not once had he even mentioned marriage or any such commitment. True, whenever he spoke, or made plans, they always included her as though she would be a part of his future, but it just wasn't the same as having him come out and state it clearly. Why, he hadn't even told her yet if he'd abandoned his previous plans, though no mention had been made of her completing another weekend vetting candidates, thank heavens! She very much doubted if she was quite up to handling that, the way she now felt about him. Perhaps she was being foolish to expect a declaration of love so soon from him, though; heaven knew, it was only one bare week since their relationship had been strung up by its heels and twisted over so dramatically. Perhaps she would just have to be a bit more patient, give him more time to accept the idea of loving her. After all, from what he'd said and from all the bits she'd deduced, love to him was an entirely new emotion, and as she knew herself it took some getting used to!

The shrill tone of the telephone ringing cut through her thoughts and, flicking off the kettle which was just starting to boil, she hurried to answer it, wondering just who could be calling so early in the day, unless it was Keir. The thought made her pulse leap with anticipation as she lifted the receiver and waited to hear is deep voice.

'Mickey?'

The voice was different—lighter and definitely not Keir's, and for a moment she failed to recognise it.

'Yes, who is this?'

'Alistair.'

Alistair! The name trickled coldly through her as though an icy finger had just slid down her spine, and she shivered. What on earth could Alistair want, phoning at this time of the morning?

'Alistair, what a surpr . . .'

'Let's cut out the pleasantries, shall we, Mickey. I want to know just what the hell you're up to.'

Gone was the usual lazy drawl he affected, replaced by a harshness and unmistakable anger which startled her into a brief, stunned silence.

'Well?' he demanded, and she hastily tried to gather her wits together. Something was obviously very wrong to make him speak to her in such a manner, but for the life of her she couldn't imagine what. Why, she'd never even spoken to the man since that lunch they'd shared with Keir, and that was several weeks ago now.

'I'm sorry, Alistair, but I'm afraid I don't know what you're talking about,' she stated firmly.

'Oh, come on, love, don't play the innocent with me. You promised me anything you came up with, and even if *that* meant nothing, I'd have thought loyalty to the paper would have stopped you going elsewhere, especially to the *Chronicle.*'

The scorn in his voice made her flinch, and just for an instant she was tempted to slam down the receiver, but she couldn't. She had to find out what he meant, although deep down she had the sudden frightening conviction she wouldn't like what he told her.

'Alistair, I've really no idea what you're talking about, so please will you tell me from the beginning?' She forced herself to speak calmly, carefully, although that first faint shiver of unease had turned into a fully-fledged shudder, which made it difficult to frame the words. There was an instant's brief hesitation, as though he was weighing up her words, and then he replied in a less aggressive tone than he'd previously used.

'There's an article in this morning's *Chronicle* on your friend, Keir Grant, about the way he is using a score system to choose the perfect wife. Are you telling me that you didn't tip them off about it?'

The words travelled down the line so clearly that they seemed to echo round and round her head; putting out her hand, Mickey grasped hold of a nearby chair as the whole room seemed to tilt and slide to the side. This just couldn't be happening, this whole nightmare conversation just couldn't really be happening! Grimly she held on to the thought, fighting off the enveloping waves of faintness with this one fragile straw, this tiny ray of hope. Surely, if she didn't move, didn't speak, didn't even breathe, then it would all disappear, fade away, become just one terrifying bad dream?

'Mickey, Mickey! Are you all right . . . Mickey?' Concern, not anger, filled Alistair's voice now, but she never heard it, every tiny part of her intent on just the one thing, keeping reality at bay. Finally, after several minutes, he cut the connection, leaving her alone with the silence.

How long she stood there Mickey never really knew, but it must have been several minutes, until slowly the insistent hum of the dialling tone whining from the receiver cut through to her fear-locked brain. Slowly, carefully, she replaced the receiver and on leaden legs crossed the room, staring out once more through the window as she tried to think, tried to understand what he had told her.

How had the paper got hold of the details? Who had told them? Who had seen Keir's notes and given them such a dreadful, vicious story? As far as she was concerned there were only two people in the world who knew what his plans had been, Keir and . . . her. What would happen when Keir heard about it? Would he believe, as Alistair had, that she'd been responsible for it?

The thought cut into her like a knife through butter, and Mickey knew that there was no time to lose; she had to get to Keir, had to speak to him, had to make him believe that never would she have done such a thing to him . . . but could she? Trust for him was such a new, fragile emotion, easily broken, easily destroyed. What if she couldn't make him believe her? What if that tiny, precious bit of trust he'd shown her by handing back the photos was just too weak to withstand such pressure? But she had to try, had to make him believe that she loved him too much to ever hurt him.

Spinning round, she ran for the door, but never made it as the phone rang again. Instinctively, she knew who was calling. Lifting the receiver, she waited, waited for the deep tones she knew she would hear, waited for the rest of the nightmare to begin.

'Why, Mickey, why did you do it?' There was no anger in his voice, just sorrow, a deep, aching sorrow which brought tears to her eyes.

'Keir, I didn't, I didn't tell them.'

'Oh, come on, Mickey, what's the point in lying about it? Even if the facts didn't speak for themselves, I've already been on to the paper, and they told me the information came from you.'

His words took her breath away, hitting her as hard as any punch, and sending her senses reeling, so that she could only repeat over and over in a mindless litany a plea that he believe her.

'I didn't, Keir, really, I didn't, I didn't.' But she doubted if he even heard her.

'I trusted you, Mickey, do you know that? I really trusted you, the first really honest woman I'd ever met, but I was wrong, wasn't I? You're like all the others, find your price and you can be bought. Well, I hope it was worth it, Mickey, I hope they paid you well. I hope it was more than thirty pieces of silver.'

Very gently he replaced the receiver, the soft click more final, more dreadful than any sound she had ever heard, and Mickey felt as though part of her had just died.

How could he believe that she'd do such an awful thing after all they'd shared that one glorious weekend and this past week? How could he believe that she was capable of such an act of viciousness, that mere money could buy her? Surely he knew how much she loved him, that the very last thing she'd ever do was to hurt him? No, deep down he must know there'd been some sort of mistake,

that she'd never be capable of such a thing. The trouble
with him was he was just too pig-headed, too hasty to
really let himself think about it, but she'd make him; she'd
make him listen, make him find out who had sold the story
to the paper, make him find out who had used her name.

Snatching up her keys, she ran out to the car and,
starting the engine, drove with a reckless speed to the flats,
as though a thousand demons were chasing her. Skidding
to a halt at the bottom of the steps, she raced inside, taking
the stairs at a pace which soon had her panting. Reaching
the door, she hammered on it with her clenched fists, the
sound echoing round and round the silent hallway time
after time as she hit it with an increasing savage fury. How
dared he ignore her, how dared he refuse to answer after
she'd just risked life and limb racing here?

Lifting up the letter-box flap, she roared crossly, 'Keir,
open this door, damn you!'

There was silence, a dreadful total silence which had her
already stretched nerves twanging. Then a voice spoke
behind her and she jumped.

'He's gone.'

'Pardon?' Swinging round, Mickey faced the elderly
porter who'd just stepped from the lift.

'Mr Grant . . . he's gone, you've missed him. You
rushed past the office before I could tell you.'

'What do you mean, he's gone? Is he out shopping?' A
strange, cold terror was pouring through her, making her
feel weak, but rigidly she held on to her control.

'Oh, no, he's gone back home, to America. Left—oh,
about twenty minutes or so ago, seemed to be in a bit of a
rush, I'd say, but then he'd left it on the late side to catch
the ten a.m. flight.' Pushing back his cuff, the man
checked his watch before stating with a grim finality, 'No,
you'll never catch him now, lass, he's gone.'

And Mickey knew he was right.

She couldn't sleep. It was three a.m., her head and body
ached with a raw tiredness, but still there was no way she
could fall asleep. Every time she closed her eyes, tried to let

her mind drift, those same words filled her head, bringing
her back to consciousness; he's gone, he's gone . . . over
and over again. Tossing back the covers, she made her way
slowly down to the kitchen.

Opening the fridge, she lifted out a carton of milk and
poured some into a pan to heat, smiling wryly to herself as
she did so. Warm milk, the age-old panacea for
sleeplessness, but she doubted if it would cure what ailed
her. For the past three days, since Keir had left, her
emotions had run the whole gamut, through sorrow,
disbelief, anger, and back again to this deep, aching
sorrow which filled her.

If only he'd waited, if only he'd trusted her enough to
wait just a little while longer and let her explain, make him
believe in her innocence. But he hadn't, and no amount of
wishing could change that one fact. Deep down Mickey
knew with an instinctive certainty that if she'd just had the
chance she could have convinced him, could have made
him realise how much she loved him and how much he
really loved her, damn him! But now he was thousands of
miles away, out of reach and there was no way she could
talk to him . . . was there?

Her eyes slid to the silent telephone, and in a flash she
knew what to do, what she should have done days before.
She'd ring him and keep on ringing him till he agreed to
listen, till he believed the truth that she told him. She loved
him, and there was no way she was letting him go out of
her life without a struggle.

Racing back upstairs, she searched along the chest of
drawers next to her bed, praying she'd still have that tissue
on which she'd jotted down his phone number, but there
was no sign of it. Wrenching open the drawers, she spilled
the contents on to the bed and scrabbled through the heap
of tumbled lingerie, till at last she found it, still screwed
into a creased little ball. She smoothed it out carefully, her
hands trembling as they pressed against the soft, pale-
tinted paper. Her whole body was shaking as though
racked with fever and, leaning her head against the
coolness of the wall for a moment, she took several deep

breaths, striving for some measure of calm. Lifting the
receiver, she started to dial carefully, eyes following the
long string of digits intently; the last thing she needed was
to get connected to some stranger.

There was a series of soft clicks and chirrups, then in a
surprisingly short time the soft, slightly alien tone of a
phone ringing, and Mickey felt her palms dampen with a
sudden flood of nervous perspiration. Now that the time
had come, was just seconds away, her mind was suddenly
a huge blank void, every one of the wonderful sentences
she'd meant to say gone, disappeared. Oh, lord, what
could she say to him?

'Hello. Keir Grant speaking.'

The deep, lovely voice came over the line, so clear that
Mickey felt she could reach out and touch him, and
suddenly a soft mist of tears sprang to her eyes, blurring
her vision.

'Hello, who is it?'

Rough impatience edged his voice now, and Mickey
knew she must answer, must find the words, the right ones
to make him listen. Opening her mouth, she started to
frame a sentence, when a second voice sounded faintly
from the receiver, faint but unmistakably female.

'Don't be long, Keir. I've got your bath ready.'

'Right, I'll be with you in a minute.'

His voice was muffled, as though he'd turned his mouth
briefly away from the receiver, and Mickey had an instant,
vivid image of him and some faceless woman about to
share the evening, if not the bath, together. The thought
knifed through her, piercing her heart with a pain which
made her stagger, made it impossible to speak. There was
a moment's pause, a brief hesitation and then he cut the
connection, and slowly Mickey replaced the receiver, and
walked back downstairs to the kitchen.

The one thing that had kept her going, held her together
these past days had been the deep-seated conviction that he
really loved her. But now, after hearing that small scrap of
conversation, she wasn't so certain. What was he doing
with another woman in his home at what must be round

seven in the evening, and a woman who was performing such an intimate task of running him a bath? Had she been a fool, a stupid, senseless fool to believe all those words he had told her? Had she really been just another conquest, another female body? Had he returned home to America, not for any reason of sorrow at her betrayal, but more from sheer pique and anger that she seemed to have beaten him?

The questions flooded her brain, as strong and as pungent as the sudden smell of burnt milk which filled the kitchen. Turning her head, Mickey watched as the white liquid oozed over the pan, to drip on to the blue flames of the burner. Putting her head in her hands, she cried, deep, racking sobs which shook her slender body; cried for the spilt milk . . . and her lost love who'd gone from her life for ever.

CHAPTER THIRTEEN

THE SOFT late-summer weather disappeared almost overnight, to be replaced by a cool, harsh greyness which only mirrored the greyness in her heart.

When Keir had first left, Mickey had been devastated, but somewhere deep inside her a tiny spark of hope that some day he'd return must have been burning. Now, with the memory of that telephone call to haunt her, that tiny spark was snuffed out and she was forced to accept the fact that it had all been one beautiful, foolish dream.

He'd never loved her, that was obvious. He'd just used her, played on her emotions to take all she'd been prepared to give him. Handing her back those photographs had meant nothing; he'd known he had a far better hold over her than any handful of prints could ever give him. He had known she loved him, and he'd traded on it. She'd been a fool to let herself get involved with a man like that, a stupid, irresponsible fool, and now she should be thanking her lucky stars that she'd found out about him; but somehow she couldn't when every single cell in her body ached for him with an insatiable hunger.

The only way she could stop herself from just sitting down and howling was to work, and she filled her days and evenings with it till she reached a state of near-exhaustion, a state Rob was quick to notice when he called round to the cottage with some proofs of the insert layout for her to check.

It had been ten days since Keir had left, ten days during which time she'd barely had ten hours' sleep, and it showed in the strained pallor of her face, the nervous twitching of her hands as she sat and studied the heap of glossy pages. Rob said nothing for several minutes, then slowly he reached forwards, lifting the pile of papers from her knee before taking her cold, nervous fingers in his warm grasp.

'Tell me, Mickey,' he said softly, and somehow she knew she must.

Gripping his hands tightly she began, the words coming from her in a jumbled, senseless torrent at first, which he found hard to follow, but slowly it all started to take shape, and he stared at her in amazement.

'And Grant really thought you'd done it, that you'd sold the story to the paper?'

'Yes,' she barely managed to whisper.

'Then he's a fool! My God, Mickey, how could he believe that?'

'I suppose it just seemed logical; only the two of us knew about his plans, and then when he rang the *Chronicle* they confirmed the story came from me.'

'Stop finding excuses for him, Mickey,' Rob said harshly. 'If he loved you, he'd know you couldn't have done such a thing, no matter what anyone told him.'

His words only reinforced what she'd been thinking for these past bitter days, and a slow river of tears slid unchecked down her cheeks as she faced it. If Keir had really and truly loved her, cared for her as she had for him, then he would have trusted her, knowing there was no way she would ever betray him.

Swearing softly at his lack of tact, Rob pulled her to him, and for a brief moment Mickey let herself rest against him, too tired to pull away. Then he gently set her from him, running a finger down the damp curve of her cheek in a light caress.

'I'm sorry love, but you have to face it,' he said gently, and she nodded.

'Yes, I know, but it still doesn't stop it hurting. I love him, Rob, so very much.'

A flash of pain twisted Rob's face, and he turned away, but not before she had time to see it, and suddenly she realised something she'd half suspected for a while now; Rob loved her. For an instant her hand lifted towards him, wanting in some way to give him comfort, till slowly she let it drop to her side.

There was nothing she could offer him, absolutely nothing which would ease the pain he was feeling. Rob loved her and she loved Keir . . . what a terrible mess!

A small silence filled the room, then Rob turned back to her slowly, all emotion blanked from his face.

'What are you going to do now, then, love?'

'What do you mean?'

Puzzled, Mickey looked up at him, not following his meaning.

'Well, are you going to fight for him, get him back?'

'Get him back . . . no, I don't think so,' she answered with a hollow laugh. 'After all, he was never really mine in the first place; all that was just an illusion.'

She'd told Rob everything except about that last desperate phone call she'd made to Keir's home, and that was still too rawly painful to mention.

'But what about whoever used your name for the story? Don't you want to know who did that?'

'I've never thought about it, but now you mention it, yes, I would like to know who hates me enough to do such a thing.' Anger was suddenly sparking inside her, making her feel more alive than she'd done for ages. Somehow, all the misery and pain she'd been feeling had overlaid the fact of just who had given the *Chronicle* the story, and now she was burning to know who it had been.

'How can I find out, though, Rob? Surely if I rang and ask I'll only get the same answer Keir did?'

'There are ways . . . just let me make a few calls and I'll see what I can come up with.'

'Of course. You go ahead while I make us a drink.'

It took a while and several phone calls before he walked through to the kitchen and, looking up, she studied his face for a few seconds before saying softly, 'Well?'

'There's no proof, of course, but word's out that a certain Angela Baddley is involved. Does the name mean anything to you?'

Mickey nodded, unable to speak, a host of images flashing into her mind: Angela seated at Keir's desk in the flat that morning; Angela at the restaurant, spitting out her threats and taunts of revenge; Angela, who hated her enough to do it. It all added up to one big total of spite.

'So now you know, are you going to tell him?' Rob asked quietly.

There was a moment's hesitation, a tiny flicker of time, when hope raced unchecked through her body, before she ruthlessly stamped it out as she answered, 'No. You see, Rob, you were quite right in what you said earlier, if he loved me he wouldn't need to be told, would he? He'd know I would never do such a thing to hurt him.'

Angela had won, done what she'd set out to do, but truthfully Mickey couldn't find it in her heart to hate her. Angela might have fired the first shot, but it had been Keir's own lack of trust which had won the battle for her.

He was tired, dog-tired and irritable. The flight had been delayed twice, once because of fog before taking off from San Francisco and now because of God knew what unforeseen circumstance on landing. He'd been reluctant to make the trip in the first place, only doing so because it was absolutely necessary for the completion of the merger, and all this hassle only added to his irritation. Now all he wanted was to get back to the flat as fast as possible, before he gave in to the almost overwhelming urge to start shouting. For the past few weeks he'd held on to his temper by the merest thread, but now he knew that thread was just about stretched to its limit. He had to get away from everyone and everything for a few hours and give himself time to think, to breathe, to sleep, and maybe in that way rid himself of this churning wave of restlessness which filled him night and day.

Forcing his way through the people, he strode rapidly across the terminal towards the exit, feeling in his pocket for the packet of cigarettes, and swearing softly when he found it empty. He'd not smoked for years till recently, but now he seemed to have started again with a vengeance, chain-smoking in an unconscious effort to quieten his raw nerves. There was no way he could get through the rest of the evening without the comfort of nicotine and, switching direction, he strode towards the shop and scooped up half a dozen packets. Turning back to pay for them, his eye caught sight of the bright poster taped to the metal news-stand and he stopped dead, the colour draining from his face. Slowly, hesitantly, he took a step forward till he was bare inches away and, reaching out, ran his fingers gently over the smooth, crisp poster paper, tracing the contours of the familiar face.

'Quite a looker, isn't she?'

The voice came from the side and, turning, Keir stared down with blank blue eyes at the elderly man standing next to him.

'The wife tries a lot of her recipes, swears by them, she does. She was really pleased when she got that little booklet in the Sunday paper yesterday, so pleased she's sent me out to get another copy to send to her sister. I've tried a few shops, but they'd all sold out, and I just thought of here and, well, looks as if I'm in luck, doesn't it? There's just one left.'

Bending, the man went to pick the thick, folded newspaper from the rack when suddenly Keir moved, snatching it up before he could touch it.

'Here! I saw that first . . .'

'I'll give you ten pounds for it,' Keir stated harshly, pulling money from his wallet and thrusting it towards him.

'Ten pounds! For a paper!' The man looked at him as though he was completely crazy, and impatiently Keir ripped out a second note and thrust it at him.

'Twenty.'

'You're on.'

With a quick flick, the man took the money and hurried off, while slowly Keir walked to the check-out and paid for his purchases. Crossing the marble-floored waiting area, he made for a row of black vinyl-covered seats and sat down, his hands trembling slightly as he pulled the booklet from the middle of the folds of paper, and stared down at the picture of Mickey on its cover. And slowly, gradually, a feeling of calm and understanding overtook him.

For weeks now, ever since that morning when he'd opened up that paper and seen the story, he'd tried to block all thought of her from his mind, as though she had never existed, but now, looking down at the familiar face, he knew he'd failed. There was no way he could wipe away the memories of her by sheer will-power, and he'd been a fool to think he could, as much of a fool as he'd been to leave so precipitously that day. He should have stayed, seen her, spoken to her, found out exactly what had made her do it and settled it, there and then. The whole reason he'd been feeling so irritable and edgy was because he'd left that whole damnable business unfinished . . . but not for much longer. He'd find Miss Michaela James and talk to her, make her explain her actions, by force if he had to!

Opening the booklet, his eyes slid grimly over the printed pages, then stopped on a short column giving a list of her forthcoming public engagements, and a faint smile curved his lips. Standing, he ripped the page from the booklet before tossing the rest of it into a nearby waste-bin and heading back towards the exit.

Miss Michaela James was about to have another addition to her audience, but one with quite a different interest in her than cooking!

'Well, I think that's it. Thank you for helping me with all this stuff.' Wearily, Mickey pushed the dark hair from her eyes, turning to smile at the two elderly women standing next to her.

'Oh, thank you, Miss James; it was such an interesting demonstration. That soufflé . . . well, what can I say? Delicious!'

'I'm glad you enjoyed it.'

Closing the boot, Mickey made her way round to the driver's door, pausing briefly to shake hands with the two ladies before sliding inside and starting the engine. Lord, she was tired! The demonstration had gone on far longer than she'd intended, but somehow she'd found it difficult to just up and leave when everyone was so eager to ask her questions. Still it was over now, and in another half-hour she'd be able to sit down and take it easy.

With a last wave she drove slowly down the narrow driveway, pulling over to hug the side of the road as a taxi turned in through the gates. Drawing level, the taxi slowed to a crawl to ease past her car, and Mickey slid an incurious glance towards it, her eyes widening in sudden horror as she caught sight of the man seated in the back. Blood rushed to her head, roared in her ears, and for one awful moment she thought she would faint!

'Mickey!'

Keir's roar did more to bring her to her senses than any amount of smelling salts could ever have done and, looking sideways Mickey felt her stomach lurch at the grim expression on his face. Panic washed through her in a sudden tide and, slamming the car into gear, she roared down the drive and swung wildly out into the road. Her heart was pounding, her mouth dry with nerves, and one thought only filled her mind . . . she had to get away!

Out on the road the traffic was mercifully light, and Mickey drove as fast as she dared, keeping one eye on her mirror, but strangely there was no sign of a pursuing car, and after a few minutes it worried her. It wasn't like him to let her go so easily with so little resistance, not like him at all . . . so what on earth was he up to?

Then suddenly the truth of the situation hit her and she groaned; why did he need to follow, to play cops and robbers, when he knew full well both where she lived and where she worked? He could track her down at any time he chose to. It wasn't a comforting thought, not one to settle her already jangling nerves; slowing the car to a crawl, Mickey gave herself time to think.

Of course, she'd been foolish to run when she'd seen him, but her reaction had been purely instinctive. If she only knew the real reason he'd sought her out, then maybe she'd know how to handle it. Still, why should she care? He'd walked out of her life two months ago now, and there was no way she was ever going to let him back in, no way she was going to let her stupid, foolish heart rule her head again!

Checking the mirror, she swooped the car into a tight curve and headed back towards town, her face grim with determination. She was going to go to ground, disappear until he left, and there was no way he was going to find her . . . ever!

'What do you mean, you can't find her! Damn it all, man, she can't just have disappeared; she's a cook, not a master criminal. She must be somewhere, you'll have to look harder!'

Slamming his fist on the desk, Keir watched as the telephone rattled. He was paying this detective a small fortune to track down Mickey, and what had he come up with? Nothing! From what the man had said, she'd disappeared off the face of the earth, and if it hadn't been for the fact that the paper was still publishing her columns he'd be convinced that something dreadful had happened to her. But no, that damned minx of a woman was hiding from him, and the hell of it was he just couldn't find her!

Rudely, he cut the man off in mid-flow and, slamming the phone down, crossed the room and poured himself a double measure of whiskey, drinking it slowly as he stared out of the window. He'd tried everything and everyone he could think of: her home, her aunt, the paper, the agency, even that damned photographer friend, Rob, but still he'd come up with absolutely nothing. No one seemed to have any clue where she was, or if they had they definitely weren't saying. Not for the first time, he rued the impulse that had made him track her down to that demonstration. At the time it had seemed like the perfect opportunity to catch her and make her explain her actions; it had never entered his head that she would take one look at him and run! Now, well, now it would probably take a wanted poster to find her.

The thought trickled through him like warm sand, found a level, then settled, and suddenly he knew he'd just hit it, the one surefire way to bring her running. Setting the glass back on the tray, he crossed the room and, pulling open the bottom drawer of his desk, slid out a rectangle of stiff paper, staring down at it for a few tense seconds. It would bring her back all right, he didn't doubt it, but the question was, would she ever forgive him?

It was a gamble, a big one, but deep down he knew he would take it.

CHAPTER FOURTEEN

SLOWING the car, Mickey stared round, checking for anything which seemed out of place, but thankfully could see nothing to alarm her. The narrow road was empty, silent in the grey hush of early morning, and with a small sigh of relief she pulled the car out of sight on to her drive. Taking the key from her pocket, she let herself in the front door and paused for a moment, as all the familiar sights and sounds of the small house poured through her like balm.

It was so good to be back, to see her own things and lock her own front door behind her. For five days now she'd felt like a fugitive, moving from one small hotel to the next, terrified to even go to Aunt Ruth's for shelter in case he found her. His determination to track her down would have surprised her if she hadn't known him so well, hadn't known how he hated to be thwarted. But thankfully, with the help of her friends, she'd managed to cover her tracks and avoid him. So far she'd won, but standing alone in the silent hallway, she wondered why it felt such a strangely empty victory.

Pushing the thought from her mind, she scooped up the bundle of letters and uncancelled papers which littered the floor and sifted through them, muttering in annoyance when she saw the *Chronicle* had been delivered for that morning. Still, it would have to do, there was no way she was going to trail down to the shop and change it. Tossing the rest of the bundle on to the hall table till she found time to deal with it later, she looked round and sighed.

Some day, some glorious day when all this was over, she'd re-do the hall and get it back into some sort of decent shape . . . some day when she just had the time.

Walking through to the kitchen, she filled the kettle and made tea, sipping at it while she skimmed through the

178

paper, barely glancing at most of the scurrilous articles it contained, until suddenly one picture caught her eye and she paused. There was something about the grainy picture which seemed vaguely familiar, and smoothing the folds out of the paper she stared intently down at it for a full minute before she realised just what she was seeing, and her whole body seemed to go cold.

It was a couple kissing, arms entwined, bodies touching, a picture which positively screamed passion . . . a picture of her and Keir! For a second it all swam out of focus, drowning in the wave of horror which engulfed her, and she had to force herself to concentrate, to read the brief caption underneath.

'Could this be it? A real 10/10 clincher for Keir Grant and the delectable Michaela James, who seems more intent on improving her score than her cooking by the look of it. Ah, well, you know the saying "the way to a man's heart . . ." '

And slowly a heated tide of horror filled her. How had it got there? Who had had it printed? Worse still, how many hundreds of people had seen it? The last time she'd seen that photograph it had been in the folder, and Keir had given that back to her, hadn't he?

A horrible, nasty suspicion crept through her, a suspicion which had her racing up to her bedroom where she'd put the folder at the bottom of a drawer, unable for these past weeks to face such a reminder of what they'd once shared. Now she dragged it out and, scattering the prints across the bed, searched for the one she'd just seen in the paper.

It wasn't there, and in one swift flash Mickey knew why he'd come back, knew just what he'd been planning. He'd threatened to have the photograph printed if she crossed him, and now he'd done it. Everything which had started on the plane had reached its final conclusion, and she realised just how big a fool she'd been to ever believe it could turn out differently. The Keir Grant she'd thought she loved had just been a myth, a disguise worn by this hard, ruthless stranger who would do anything and hurt anybody if it suited his plans. He'd used her from start to finish—used her, never loved her. Snatching the photos up, she tore them into a thousand tiny pieces, as tiny as the pieces of her smashed heart.

Tears were streaming down her cheeks in hot, bitter torrents, but she scarcely felt them, overwhelmed by a sudden wild grief at this final evidence of how little he had cared for her. The thought gnawed at the edge of her grief insistently, slowly working through to the centre and gradually turning it to a deep, burning anger; anger at herself for being so foolish, and anger at him for what he'd done to her and she knew that there was no way she could live with herself unless she told him exactly what she thought of his actions.

Brushing the tears from her cheeks, she turned to go, pausing as a thought struck her; bending down she gathered up the tiny scraps of photographs and shoved them back into their folder. She'd valued these pictures, seen them as a token of so much, but now she knew that all along they'd been worthless, as worthless as the man who had given them to her. She would give them back to him, every single last scrap—give them back and break the link between them for ever.

The morning traffic was heavy, and Mickey drove with an intense concentration, terrified of having an accident before she could speak to him, before she could tell him what a pathetic piece of humanity he had turned out to be. Parking the car at the driveway of the flats, she made her way inside and knocked on the door, standing stiff and unsmiling as it swung open.

'Mickey!'

Stunned, Keir could only stare at her in astonishment for a second, flinching back as she spoke.

'I won't ask you why you did it, Keir, there's no point—after all, you did warn me. I just wanted to say I would never have believed anyone could be so vicious as to do such a thing. You're despicable, Keir Grant, do you know that? Totally despicable, and the pity of it is I really and honestly thought you were the man I wanted to spend the rest of my life with, but then that shows you what a fool I was, doesn't it? Now, well, now I'm rather glad you had that picture published; it means it's all finally over. You've done your worst, so you've no more hold over me and I'm just going to tell you this once . . . stay out of my life, Keir, I don't need you, stay out of it for ever.'

Turning to go, she paused as a sudden thought struck her and, upending the envelope, watched as the tiny fragments of paper fluttered round his feet like sad confetti. Then, staring up into his face for one brief, silent second, she stated sadly, 'You might as well have these back, they're as worthless as you.'

Her words cut into him, stunning him with their bitter sadness and anger so that for an instant he could only watch as she walked along the corridor to the lift. Then suddenly his senses returned with a flash; she was leaving, after all he'd gone through to find her she was walking away, and he was standing there letting her!

'Mickey! Come back here,' he roared grimly, but she ignored him, stepping into the lift and pressing the button for the ground floor. With a muttered curse he headed for the stairs, and raced down them, uncaring that he was only wearing the short towelling robe he'd slipped on after his shower. There was no way that damned woman was going to elude him again!

Stepping from the lift, Mickey walked towards the doors, feeling strangely limp now that all the anger was draining away. She felt hollow, empty, as though someone had just scooped out a great part of her soul and tossed it aside, and just for a second she wondered how she could ever manage to live in a world which no longer held Keir . . . at least, not for her.

'Mickey, stop!'

The shout startled her into obedience, and she shot a quick look over her shoulder at the tall figure who'd arrived at the bottom of the stairs. For the first time she noticed just what he was wearing—which, frankly, was very little. The short brown robe gaped open, revealing more of his tanned torso and legs than it covered, and colour flooded her pale cheeks at the sight of him. Hastily she turned away, refusing to be drawn into any argument in the middle of the foyer with him in that state.

'I said wait.'

How dared he? Just who did he think he was, to issue orders after all she'd just said? Spinning round, she snapped nastily, 'I don't give a damn what you said, and don't you dare shout at me.'

'I'll shout if I need to, you stubborn woman. I want to talk to you.' Reaching out, he grabbed her shoulder.

Mickey's reaction was instinctive, the result of long years of training as, shifting her weight, she tossed him sideways, watching with a dawning horror as he hit the floor with a thump and lay completely still. My God, what had she done? Had she killed him? Falling to her knees, she ran her hand over his face and down his neck, feeling the steady tap of his pulse with a rush of relief which made her feel almost faint. Leaning forwards, she rested her forehead against the hardness of his shoulder.

'What happened?'

His voice was low, shaky, still blurred with the impact of his fall; sitting up, she ran a gentle hand down the side of his face in a soothing gesture.

'Shhh—you'll be all right in a moment. Just get your breath back. You—er—you had a fall.'

'A fall . . .' Slowly, remembrance returned to the blue eyes, and Mickey winced as she waited for his anger, but strangely none came. Reaching up, he pulled her to him and hugged her, while laughter shook his big frame.

'You devil, you threw me, didn't you?'

The blow must have caused more damage than she'd thought, to bring about this sort of reaction, and pulling back, Mickey stared at him in alarm, something fluttering in her chest when she saw the expression in his blue eyes, but she ignored it. Her main concern must be to get him to a doctor; the floor was of marble and he'd hit it with quite a crack. It was no wonder he was acting so strangely. Settling her face into a crisply sensible expression, she started to speak. 'Look, Keir, I think you should . . .'

'Oh!'

The scream rang shrilly across the empty foyer, making her jump, and for an instant she moved closer to Keir, as though for protection. Turning her head, she caught sight of the two elderly ladies who'd just walked through the door, and suddenly realised from the shocked expressions of their faces just what they must look like, lying on the floor together with him barely dressed. A crimson tide of embarrassment flooded her cheeks, and she stumbled to her feet, uncaring that her elbow caught him a glancing blow on the chin, sending his already delicate senses reeling. She had to get away.

'Mickey!'

He sounded so helpless lying there, blue eyes hazy, that for an instant she wavered. It was all he needed. Grasping her hand, he hauled himself slowly to his feet, quickly adjusting the gaping robe, which was doing very little to cover his modesty, and thought quickly. The two women were standing by the lift, backs turned determinedly towards them; linking his fingers in Mickey's Keir said softly, 'Will you help me back upstairs to the flat? I don't think they'd appreciate sharing the lift with me at the moment.'

How could she refuse? Cheeks still pink with embarrassment, Mickey nodded and let him put his arm round her shoulders to help him back up the stairs. Pushing open the door to his flat, she led him inside, pausing, undecided where to take him, when he said faintly, 'I think I'd better lie down, don't you?'

He still sounded dreadfully shaky, and though every instinct screamed at her to refuse she found herself helping him through to his bedroom and settling him down on the huge bed. Closing his eyes, he ran a hand over his forehead, as though in pain, and anxiously she bent towards him, her breath stirring the soft, streaked hair on his forehead.

'Keir, shall I call a doctor?'

The hand reached out, and in a flash he'd pulled her

down beside him, trapping her body against the mattress with his. Looking up, Mickey could see no hint of weakness in the eyes which were burning down at her like blue flames, and knew that he'd tricked her . . . yet again.

'Let me go! Let me go, damn you!'

Struggling, she tried to free herself, but he wouldn't let her, keeping her pressed tight against his body to stop her moving, and gradually she realised that all her struggles were causing the completely wrong sort of reaction. She went limp, looking up at him with sad hazel eyes which were misted with tears.

'Don't do this, Keir,' she whispered softly.

'Don't do what?' He spoke gently, carefully lifting the glasses from her face so that he could kiss her eyes closed, because the expression in them was haunting.

'Don't make me want you.'

'Can I?'

Staring down at her, he waited for her answer, a sudden tension to his body which she couldn't understand, and she turned her head away, unable to bear to see the triumph in his eyes when she answered.

'Yes.'

The word was low, a soft sigh of sound. Leaning forwards, he caught the echo of it on his lips as he kissed her. There was an instant's hesitation, a tiny flicker of time when she tried to remember what he'd done and how she hated him, then it was gone, wiped away by the magic of his lips.

The kiss was slow, tender, strangely healing, and when it was over Keir looked down at her soft face and said quietly, gently as though he'd just made a discovery which stunned him, 'I love you.'

The words stole what little was left of her breath away, so that for a moment she could only stare up into his handsome face in wonder. He loved her! He'd actually said he loved her . . . but could she believe him?

Swiftly her eyes ran over the hard planes of his face, searching desperately for something which would allow this tiny flame of hope which had ignited inside her to grow, and she found it; found it in the soft curve of his lips, in the deep blue glow which shone in his eyes. He loved her, he'd said so, and now she didn't doubt it.

Reaching up, she slid her arms around his neck to pull him slowly down, so that their lips met in a tender, gentle kiss. Although Mickey knew there were hundreds and thousands of questions which must be answered, none of them mattered just at the moment. He loved her and she love him, and she could build her life on that knowledge.

She kissed him with every tiny bit of the pent-up longing she'd felt these past lonely weeks, and suddenly all the gentleness disappeared, burnt away by the great roar of passion which engulfed them, the burning need to seal their love in this age-old way.

They made love urgently: hands, lips, bodies, touching, meeting, fusing in an intense desperation, as though only in this way could they rid each other of their pain. As Mickey, suddenly caught up in the moment of completion, called his name, she heard him echo it with hers. Later, her head cushioned against the hardness of his shoulder, dark hair curling wildly across his skin in silken strands, Keir knew that he had just found everything he'd been searching for, and smoothed a kiss over each of her closed lids in gentle adoration.

Opening her eyes, Mickey stared up at him for one long moment, then, raising her hand, ran it gently down the lean curve of his cheek as she whispered softly, 'I love you, Keir, now and for ever,' and saw the sudden emotion which crossed his face and flooded the blue eyes with a mist of alien tears. In one swift movement he crushed her to him and held her, saying nothing, just held her as he tried to get himself back under control. When he spoke his voice was low, husky with feeling.

'I don't deserve you to love me, Mickey, after all I've done to you.'

And Mickey knew that now was the time they must speak, must clear away all the old hurts and fears which had lain between them these long weeks. Inching herself back, she looked up into his face and said quietly, 'I didn't give the story to the papers, Keir.'

'I know,' he said quietly, his eyes intent as they studied her face.

'You do! How?' Startled, she stared up at him.

'It was last night; I was sitting here, tossing the whole mess round in my mind, when suddenly I just realised that there was no way you were capable of such a vicious act. The one thing that had always struck me right from the start was your honesty and there was no way I could see you planning such an underhand trick. It got me thinking, something I should have done weeks ago; if you hadn't done it, then who had?'

'And did you work it out?' she asked softly.

'Yes,' he replied his face grim,' Oh, yes, once I'd cleared my mind of all that foolishness about you betraying me, then I soon worked out who it had been . . . Angela?'

Mickey nodded, too full of emotion to find any words to speak. That he'd finally trusted her enough to believe in her innocence overwhelmed her.

Leaning forwards, he pressed a gentle kiss to her lips.

'I'm sorry, Mickey. If I'd been half-way rational at the time I would have realised you could never do such a thing, but when I opened the paper and saw that article, something inside me just seemed to snap. You see, honey, all my life I've learned not to trust other people, and especially women, so that . . .' He stumbled, as though unable to find the right words to continue.

'So that it was natural to believe I'd betrayed you,' she finished quietly for him, hating to hear the anguish in his deep voice.

'Yes, I'm afraid so. I'm sorry for doubting you, but I'd never met anyone like you before; a woman who was kind, tender, caring, not just out for all she could get. It threw me.'

Sitting up, he packed a pillow behind his back, keeping his face averted, as though it hurt him to tell her how he'd formed such an opinion over the years. Gently Mickey slid her hand into his, and felt him grip it tightly before he continued, 'All my life I've seen women who've been willing to do anything for money, starting with my mother. She left because she'd had a better offer, a guy with more money than my father, and she didn't give a damn about leaving us, didn't care what happened. She saw her chance and took it. And then there was Karen.'

'Your sister?'

'Yes, my sister.' His fingers tightened to that Mickey had to force herself not to wince with the unconscious pain he was inflicting. 'My sister . . . the sister I'd cared for all those years. Do you know what she did? Do you, Mickey?'

'No.'

'She sold herself to any man who wanted her. She's a hooker, Mickey, a goddam hooker!'

The words exploded from him, and Mickey rested her head against his shoulder, wishing there was some way she could give him comfort for such pain. The wounds were deep, old, and, from the tone of his voice, still hurting, but deep down Mickey knew she could heal them, could wipe away the pain with her love. Turning her head, she pressed a gentle kiss to the warm flesh of his shoulder, feeling the way his muscles flickered in an instinctive reaction to her touch, and said softly, 'It's all over now, though, Keir. I'll never hurt you like that. I love you too much.'

Her voice was warm with sincerity and conviction and, looking down at her, he smiled, feeling the last of the ice which had encased his heart these long, lonely years shatter.

'No, I know you won't. I'm sorry about that picture in the paper, but I was desperate, Mickey. I'd nearly ripped the town apart, and still couldn't find you.'

'Yes, I did a good job, didn't I?' she replied smugly, loving the way his eyes roved over her face, as though storing up details.

'Very good,' he agreed drily. 'But I knew that photo would bring you running.'

'Why did you keep it, Keir? Didn't you trust me enough to give them all back? At the time I felt that you did, but later . . .'

'Oh, no, it wasn't that at all. Frankly, after that night we'd shared together I knew there was no way I could ever use them against you. It was just an impulse, to keep one so that I'd have a reminder of you, something to look at when you weren't there.'

There was no doubting the sincerity in his deep voice, and she smiled.

'If only we'd spoken sooner, then most of this would never have happened, would it?'

Suddenly she remembered the phone call she'd made to America, and the woman's voice she'd overheard, and a tiny flicker of jealousy arose in a sudden flash, making her say quickly, 'I rang you, one evening.'

'In America? You did? But . . .'

'You answered, but then I heard a woman's voice in the background; something about running you a bath and I . . . thought you had found someone else.'

There it was, out into the open, and she stared up at him, waiting for an answer, the tension easing from her as she saw him smile.

'Someone else? Oh, Mickey, you idiot, that was my housekeeper. How on earth could there ever be anyone else? You, lady, are a hard act to follow!'

'Do you think so?' she asked, her voice teasing.

'I know so. Oh, I knew you affected me right from the very beginning, but I fought against it. When I look back, I think I was half-way in love with you from the first time I kissed you. I know it completely knocked me for six. Then later, after that first disastrous weekend, I kept wondering if I was doing the right thing by using the scores, when you seemed so certain I was making such a mistake. You made me undecided, uncertain, unable to make a decision and stick to it . . . something which had never happened to me before, I can tell you. All I knew was that you made me feel strangely protective towards you, and guilty as hell for all the anguish I was putting you through.'

'Good,' she said, laughing up at him. 'You deserved to suffer; you had me worried stiff, what with all your threats and with the way I was starting to feel about you.'

'Oh, I suffered all right, believe me, especially when I saw that guy Rob with you that day in the car park. Heaven knows how I managed to stop myself from rushing over and hitting him when I saw you kiss him!'

'And I thought you were angry because I'd suddenly appeared and I was the last person you wanted to see,' she said softly.

'Far from it,' he said with a low self-mocking laugh. 'No, I was well and truly hooked by then, lady, but just too stubborn to admit it. Now, though, I've no intention of being a fool any longer. There's no way I'm ever going to let you go again, Mickey; I want to marry you . . . if you'll have me.'

The low, delicious voice rumbled softly across the few inches which separated them, and Mickey felt her toes begin to curl as they'd done all those weeks before when she'd first heard it. Slithering closer, she settled herself against his warm body, her hand running lightly over the smooth skin of his chest in a tantalising caress.

'Oh, I'll have you all right! I think I'll have to when Aunt Ruth sees that compromising photo in the paper. She might be old, but I have the feeling she could still hold a shotgun steady if she wanted to.'

Keir chuckled. 'I hope that isn't the only reason, honey.'

'No, it isn't. I love you, Keir, more than I can find the words to tell you, but are you sure, absolutely sure I'm the one you want?'

There was no mistaking the invitation in her eyes and, smiling, Keir slid down to answer it, his hand trailing lazily over the delicate bones of her neck and shoulders, and downwards in a slow touch of fire which made her quiver with longing. Bending his head, he stared deep into her eyes for a long moment, then said softly, 'I'm sure, Mickey, absolutely certain. There'll never be anyone else but you. I've made my final score and it's perfect.' And gently, he kissed her.

You'll flip . . . your pages won't!
Read paperbacks *hands-free* with

Book Mate · I

The perfect "mate" for all your romance paperbacks

Traveling • Vacationing • At Work • In Bed • Studying • Cooking • Eating

Perfect size for all standard paperbacks, this wonderful invention makes reading a pure pleasure! Ingenious design holds paperback books OPEN and FLAT so even wind can't ruffle pages – leaves your hands free to do other things. Reinforced, wipe-clean vinyl-covered holder flexes to let you turn pages without undoing the strap . . . supports paperbacks so well, they have the strength of hardcovers!

Pages turn WITHOUT opening the strap.

SEE-THROUGH STRAP

Reinforced back stays flat.

Built in bookmark.

BOOK MARK

BACK COVER HOLDING STRIP

10" x 7¼", opened.
Snaps closed for easy carrying, too.

Available now. Send your name, address, and zip code, along with a check or money order for just $5.95 + .75¢ for postage & handling (for a total of $6.70) payable to Reader Service to:

Reader Service
Bookmate Offer
901 Fuhrmann Blvd.
P.O. Box 1396
Buffalo, N.Y. 14269-1396

Offer not available in Canada
*New York and Iowa residents add appropriate sales tax.

BM-G